THE FALL AND RISE OF HENRY MILCH

A WYANDOT COUNTY MYSTERY

MARSHALL THORNTON

Published by Kenmore Books

Edited by Joan Martinelli

Cover design by Marshall Thornton

Images by 123rf stock

ISBN: 979-8-9902397-0-8

First Edition

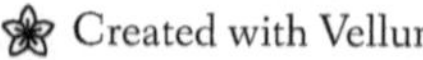 Created with Vellum

ACKNOWLEDGMENTS

I'd like to thank Tina Greene-Bevington, Nathan Bay, Chris Carter, Jennie Evenson, Ben Thompson, Shanee Edwards, Danielle Wolff, and, of course, my editor Joan Martinelli.

CHAPTER ONE

I... wait for it, drumroll please, I... bought a car. And it is perfect! A convertible. Okay, I'll admit that may be a little impractical for Northern Lower Michigan, particularly in the winter, particularly because there's a tiny little rip over the backseat covered in several pieces of black gaffer's tape. What is a gaffer, anyway? Clearly someone who uses enough black tape to get it named after them.

Whatever.

My car. Honestly, it's a joy to say those words. My car, my car, my car. My car is a 1992 Geo Metro convertible in a very bright blue. I don't know what they called it in the original brochure, but I would call it Popsicle Blue. You know, a blue that reminds you of artificial food coloring. Totally cool.

It has a three-cylinder engine with fifty-some horsepower and a five-speed manual transmission. It's a blast to drive since you have to slam your foot down on the accelerator and keep it there regardless of what gear you're in.

I do know how to drive a five-speed. FYI: My Honda CRX was a five-speed. So, my occasional grinding of the gears was due to navigating the subtle differences between the gear boxes rather than any lack of understanding on my part.

The car cost thirty-two hundred dollars, and then another two-hundred and fifty-five when it had to go immediately into the shop. And then there were registration fees and car insurance, so needless to say my bank account was once again on life support.

Worse, the ER bill had arrived for my visit last spring after I was run off the road while trying to solve Sammy Hart's murder and get the reward his friends offered. My Nana Cole intercepted the bill and stupidly paid it. Then she told me I owed her the more than four thousand dollars it had cost. I was furious.

"First of all, don't open my mail. Second of all, why would you pay that bill?"

My nana was somewhere around seventy, with gray hair that she wore in a style she'd chosen sometime in the nineteen-fifties. She was small, had brown eyes, and had suffered a stroke in the spring which still affected her ability to walk—mainly because she refused physical therapy.

"You were taken care of," she said. "They deserve to be paid."

"I was in a car accident which was not my fault."

Okay, that was problematic since the car involved belonged to a dead person and the driver who'd attempted to run me off the road was in jail awaiting trial. So it wasn't exactly an accident, it was more attempted murder. Something I'm sure insurance companies balked at paying. None of which means *I'm* the one who should pay my ER bill.

"Don't you understand?" I said. "You never ever pay a medical bill."

"It will ruin your credit."

"My credit *is* ruined."

"Well, you'll need credit someday. When the farm is yours."

"And at that point I'll pay my medical bills. Not to

mention, if the farm is going to be mine someday why do I have to pay you back?"

"Because it's not yours yet and it builds character."

Honestly, what *is* character anyway? People only seem to bring it up when they want you to do things their way. And, really, wouldn't it be more character building to do things your own way? Wouldn't that teach you something about who you are?

"If you want your money, you should sue your cousin Rupert Beckett, Jr. He's the one who ran me off the road."

"Allegedly. That hasn't been proven in court."

Frustrated, I went upstairs to my bedroom (formerly my mother's bedroom) and grabbed my lime green iBook off the French provincial desk, climbed onto the twin bed while nudging my yellow dog, Reilly to one side. Immediately, he moved back, pressing himself against my leg. I looked at him as if he was insane—it was too hot for puppy cuddles. I considered pushing him off the bed, but... Anyway, I decided to just ignore my now sweaty leg and flipped open my laptop. I surfed the 'Net until I found out how much home healthcare workers made.

It was shockingly low, sometimes as little as seven dollars an hour. I decided my rate was ten dollars an hour. Yes, I had absolutely no experience taking care of anyone, even myself, but I did have a college education (BA Communications, UCLA, 2001) and I believe the ability to converse intelligently about things I know nothing about to be worth an extra three dollars an hour.

Therefore, I'd taken care of my Nana Cole for eight weeks at sixty hours a week. Four hundred- and eighty-dollars times eight was forty-six hundred dollars. Notice I was nice enough not to charge overtime. Well, she is family after all. In total, she actually owed me several hundred dollars more than she said I owed her. I typed up an invoice and printed it out. Then I brought it downstairs and gave it to her.

"What is this?"

"It's an invoice for taking care of you."

"You did that because we're family."

"Which would be a reason for you to pay my medical bill and not ask to be reimbursed."

"It's not the same thing."

"You're right. It's the not the same. You owe me more."

"I'm not paying it."

"But it would be character building if you did."

Needless to say, it was a stalemate. And I was broke.

Which is how I ended up back at the Wyandot County Land Conservancy. They were quite busy and, according to my Nana Cole's close friend Bev, really needed me. The thing that confused me was that the entire point of the organization was to do nothing—land was put under conservancy meaning that it could not be sold for development or farming or anything really. No one was to do anything to the land. The whole point was to do nothing. So why were they busy? What did they actually have to do?

Anyway, Bev asked I come with her to a farm, which was almost in Leelanau County for God's sake. I offered to drive. Well, insisted is probably a better description. I clinched the deal by saying, "Seriously, the car gets almost forty miles to the gallon. Isn't it better for the environment if I drive?" Bev's Jeep Cherokee was from the '80s and got as close to zero miles per gallon as you could possibly get. She didn't have a leg to stand on.

So there we were chugging along with the top down. Fortunately, it was a lovely day with the temperature close to eighty—in September, no less. It's important to note that a Michigan eighty is approximately an L.A. hundred and one. That's how much difference humidity makes. A surprise to me.

It was so warm that even with the top down I was tempted to turn on the air conditioning. I didn't because I knew that would make it nearly impossible for the car to top forty-five miles an hour. As it was, we were having trouble reaching the sixty-five mile an hour speed-limit on the backwoods roads.

Bev Jenkins was around sixty, with short-cropped salt-and-pepper hair which actually flattered her. I hadn't yet figured her out. On the one hand, I was certain she'd be a hit at the Palms, a super famous lesbian bar in Los Angeles. On the other hand, she might just be the kind of straight woman who never fully understood that a flannel shirt, a square figure and a sunbaked complexion were not the way to a man's heart.

"We're going to the Flaherty farm. A hundred acres. Mostly corn, sunflower seeds, hay. They've also got a modest-sized dairy, so they keep a portion of the corn and hay they grow for feed."

Why she thought I'd be interested in that was beyond me.

"They have about twenty acres of wetlands they're putting under conservancy because they really can't use the land."

"What about rice? Don't you grow rice on a wetland?"

Seriously, I watch a lot of TV.

"You do, but I think you need a man-made wetland you can flood at will and much higher temperatures than we have in Michigan."

A funny thing to say on a day when it was nearly eighty degrees and massively humid. I shrugged.

The whole giving away your land thing didn't make a lot of sense to me. Firstly, because you didn't actually give it away, you just promised to never use it in a particular way and that earned you a huge tax break. Still, though, if I owned land, even the crappy kind you couldn't do much with, I wouldn't want to just give it away. Promise or no.

Come to think of it, I might someday own land and be faced with exactly that choice. No, I didn't believe that would happen. I didn't trust my grandmother for a minute. She specifically said she was going to leave me the farm so that I didn't go back to Los Angeles and die a drug addict. She thought my staying in Michigan and being a farmer was the best thing for me. It was not.

No, I had every intention of going back to Los Angeles and *not* dying of a drug overdose. Presumably that would mean I was out of the will. Oh, well.

Yes, I had realized that my drug use had gotten a tad out of hand. And I was taking steps to get a handle on that. I was currently titrating down. I'd guesstimated my daily usage (higher than I'd like to admit) and am now carefully taking much less. Every week. Step by step. Very soon now I was going to be a completely not-addicted person. A week maybe. Possibly a month. Very soon, though.

Anyway, I pulled into the Flaherty farm and drove down their long, long driveway. The house was similar to my grandmother's, except that it didn't have a porch made of river rock. No, their porch was boring old wood. Next to the house was a gigantic, well-weathered barn.

As we got out of the car, Bev stood back and looked the car over, then said, "You know it has a shimmy, don't you?"

"I'm sure it's deliberate. I think they wanted to create a feeling of suspense."

"I don't think suspense is what people want to feel when they're driving," Bev said.

"It's a niche market."

And then Jimmy Flaherty came out of the house and headed over to us. He was a bald man in his late fifties, maybe? It was hard to tell. He was thin and had a pronounced curve in his spine. If he turned sideways, he'd look like a question mark. Bald *and* a hunchback. If that's what farming did to you, I wanted no part of it.

He knew Bev, so they just said hello and how are you. Then she introduced me. "This is my colleague, Henry Milch."

"Mooch," I said, earning myself a sharp look from Bev.

Alright, I suppose it's not a very professional name, but I did sort of like it. Not that anyone ever used it.

Jimmy Flaherty looked me up and down—as well he should. I was wearing one of my fav outfits: overall shorts with a lime green wifebeater and a pair of ankle high work boots. It was the perfect day-to-night outfit. If I were going out all I needed to do was take off the wifebeater, unclip one of the straps and presto chango I was ready for whatever life brought my way.

God, I missed L.A.

"Henry Milch," Jimmy Flaherty said. "You the one who put the two Ruperts in jail?" He meant Rupert Beckett, Jr. and Rupert Beckett, Sr. who'd killed Sammy Hart.

"Technically, the sheriff put them in jail."

"But aren't they your cousins?"

"They're related to my grandmother."

"That makes them your cousins."

"I don't like to think of them that way. They tried to murder me; twice. Kind of puts a damper on the whole idea of a family reunion."

He looked at me like it was hard to accept what I'd just said. Finally he mumbled, "Maybe so, maybe so."

"So, Jimmy," Bev said. "Why don't you take us out to these wetlands we've been talking about. I want Henry to see them. He'll be coming out with a surveyor next week to get the exact description of the property you want under conservancy."

That was news to me. And apparently to Jimmy. He gave me a nasty look. One I'd seen before.

"And you'll let the tax man know?" he asked Bev.

"No, actually, I think you'll need to file those documents yourself. But we'll give you copies of everything you need."

He grumbled a little—apparently, he was expecting a full-service charitable organization—then he led us out into a wide field behind the house. He stopped and pointed in one direction. "There's a rebar post just at the tree line over that way.

Then another that way. You'll be using the Olms brothers, I expect?"

"Niles Olms, yes," Bev said.

"Well, he knows the land I'm talking about. You don't need to send anyone. He can come alone."

"There should be someone from the conservancy here during the survey."

"Yeah? Then you come."

"Jimmy, you can't decide who the conservancy sends," Bev said.

"It's okay," I said. "I'm sure I have better things to do."

Bev stared at me for a moment, then her expression turned grateful. I'd solved the conflict for her.

"Fine," she said, before the two of them began talking about random people they both knew.

Perhaps, Jimmy didn't want me around because he was close friends with my murderous cousins. But I doubted that. No, I knew why he didn't want me around. Things like this happened with some regularity in Wyandot County. Not that they didn't happen in L.A. But having kids yell 'Fag' at you from a moving car was much less personal than being told face-to-face not to come back.

Bev suggested we walk back up to the house. They kept chatting, and when we got close Jimmy brought up an afford-able housing project they'd proposed for Masons Bay, saying, "I don't understand what that phrase is supposed to mean. If housing isn't affordable then no one will buy it. All housing is affordable to someone."

Bev decided to politely disagree, so I wandered back to my car. I had a purpose, of course. I knew Bev had left her bag in the car. I knew that she had a Valium prescription due to what was an apparently mild case of epilepsy. I was hoping she'd recently had her prescription refilled so that I could nab a couple.

From where I was, I could hear snippets of their conversation. Bev was saying everyone deserved housing, while Jimmy was implying poor people didn't want to work. My answer to that was let's see him make six caramel macchiatos in a row. Not that I missed being a barista. In fact, it was probably the only thing I didn't miss about L.A.

As I poked through Bev's purse, I made a mental note to think about what other kind of survival job I could get when I got back to West Hollywood. I had a decent education, so I could probably get a job as someone's assistant. What would that be—oh, I found the pills. And, yay, she'd recently had them refilled. It was good that she was taking care of herself. I took four and slipped them into a pocket, then put the bottle back.

Obviously, it was not the first time I'd accepted Bev's unwitting generosity. But now, I really needed the Valium. Titrating down from a very minor Oxy addiction had its prickly moments, and a Valium here or there helped me through the worst of it. I really hoped Bev wasn't good at counting, since I would probably have to snag some more in a week or so.

Anyway... She came back to the car and got in.

"I'm sorry about that," she said.

"Sorry about what?"

"That he didn't want you to come back."

"No problem. He's not my type anyway."

She was trying to be nice, and I appreciated that. I mean, not enough to feel bad about taking pills from her purse. But enough to think I should probably pay her back sometime—not in Valium, of course, but someday I'd do something nice for her. If it was easy.

She said, "I shouldn't have argued with him, that's not the way to get people to give you donations."

"I don't think he gave you a donation. I think he got his taxes reduced."

"You have a point. Still, that's a bad habit I shouldn't get into."

We were quiet again as I turned around and drove back down Jimmy Flaherty's driveway. Once I was back on County Road 669, she asked, "How is your grandmother?"

"Annoying," I replied over the whining of my engine and the howl of wind coming over the windshield.

"She's her old self then. Good. Have you heard from your mother?"

"My mother? Not for a while. She's yachting."

"I know it's not my business, but do you know why your mother doesn't get along with Emma?"

"They hate each other?"

"Yes, but is there a reason?"

I could have sworn I'd just given her the reason: They hate each other. I shrugged dramatically and said, "You know, they've always been like that. As long as I can remember."

She said, "Hmmph," as though she didn't believe me. I guess I could have said it probably had something to do with her running off with Pauly Milch when she was seventeen. Pauly Milch was my not-father. They'd gone their separate ways well before I was conceived. I didn't say that though, because I assumed she'd ask a million questions and I did not have a million answers.

"What time is it?" I asked.

Bev glanced at her watch and said, "It's nearly twelve thirty."

"Okay. I have a one o'clock doctor's appointment, so I'll drop you off at the office and go over. I probably won't be out until around two and I didn't get a lunch hour. Do I really need to come back?"

Yeah, yeah, yeah, I was stretching things. Actually, my visits with Dr. Blinski took a whole ten minutes, max. He'd ask if my ankle was still bothering me, and I'd say it was even though it wasn't, and he'd refill my Oxy prescription. And, of course, charge me seventy-five dollars, cash.

Bev didn't need to know any of that.

The rest of the trip Bev talked about all the things she wanted me to do next week. I stopped paying attention and wished I could put in a CD. The car had a pretty decent Pioneer stereo the previous owner had very wisely installed, and I was—as always—obsessed with Kylie Minogue's album, *Fever*. It reminded me of home (yes, home is a gay dance club), so I played it constantly. Seriously, 'Can't get you out of my head' ... Fabulous song. There was so much I couldn't get out of my head.

Bev was barely out of the car when I popped in the CD.

"See you on Monday," she said.

I guess I was working on Monday.

Dr. Blinski's office was the front half of a house with a river rock façade on the edge of downtown Masons Bay. A few blocks away was the bustling (in the summer) tourist shopping area, which included several restaurants, a couple of boutique clothing shops, a coffee shop called Cuppa Mud, the bookstore, two fudge shops, a bakery and a hairdresser.

I got a parking space almost right in front. I jumped out of my convertible—I mean, I opened the door. I tried jumping into the car once in my grandmother's driveway and will not be doing that again.

Walking into the lobby of Dr. Blinski's office—which had once been the front porch and had the windows to prove it—I went right up to the sliding window next to the reception desk. His nurse-slash-secretary was a gray-haired woman in her forties named Nancy Fisher, who I'd gotten to know a little bit given that I'd been in the office several times a month, either for my grandmother or for myself. Dr. Blinski didn't give refills, so I was there twice a month to replenish my supply.

Nancy had to know what was going on. The more often I came the less she looked me in the eye. When I'd first come, she'd led me back to the doctor's office, helped me get onto the exam table, and then took my vitals. After a couple of visits, she'd stopped doing that and would just send me back. I guess it had stopped being important that my heart was still beating.

The indirect looks she gave me were frosty and unfriendly. I guess I couldn't blame her. If I'm being honest—and I try not to be, believe me—my visits to Dr. Blinski were little more than drug deals. It wasn't surprising that Nancy Fisher might want to distance herself from that as much as possible. Which did not stop me from smiling at her and asking how she was and then asking after her pregnant daughter who'd just married, scandal of scandals, a Black man. She'd give sharp, one-word answers like 'fine' and 'good.'

That morning she took one look at me and said, "You can go back."

Dr. Blinski's office was very homey with an oak rolltop desk and an old-fashioned exam table. I was expecting to walk in and climb onto the exam table so we could have our little chat. Instead, I opened the door, took one step in, and fell down. I think I might have grunted or groaned or swore when I did. It took a moment to realize I'd fallen on top of Dr. Blinski and was now staring into his hair-filled ear canal. I attempted to push myself up, but my arm slid out from under me.

Blood, a great deal of it, all over the floor, all over Dr. Blinski, and now, all over me. Using my other hand, I found a dry spot and pushed myself off the doctor. I stood up and tried to take it all in.

A scalpel rested in the middle of a lake of blood. His head was turned to the right, exposing a two-to-three-inch wound which clearly cut through an important artery. I knew the artery had a name—I knew it once for about thirty-six hours when I took an anatomy class. I needed two lab sciences to get my degree and—anyway, not important now.

The doctor's throat was cut. Though he was clearly dead, I

reached down and tried to take his nonexistent pulse. Dead, but still warm.

Looking around the room, I noticed a drawer open in the desk, some papers had fallen to the floor, and it looked like there might have been a struggle. Or maybe the doctor was just messy. I couldn't be sure.

I also noticed that the window was open and there were several fingertip-shaped blood smears on the sill. It seemed obvious the killer had gone out the window. I took a step closer to get a better look when there was an ear-piercing howl behind me.

I turned to see, Nancy Fisher standing there screaming, and she seemed to have no intention of stopping.

CHAPTER TWO

Two hours later, I was sitting in an interview room in the sheriff's office at the Wyandot County Municipal Center waiting for Detective Rudy Lehmann to come in and talk to me. I was absolutely distraught. Lehmann had insisted on taking my clothes as "evidence," which left me sitting there in his gym clothes: a pair of red nylon running shorts and a gray T-shirt from the Tip Top Tap, a local cidery. I kept sniffing myself. I had the horrible feeling he'd gone to the gym that morning.

"When do I get my clothes back?" I'd asked, as I handed them over.

"No idea."

"Okay, well, bloodstains are super hard to get out and the longer you wait... Could you possibly rinse the overalls out in cold water? Also, salt. I've heard that works."

"The blood is the whole point."

That didn't make any sense and it wasn't until a while later, after he'd left me alone in the interview room for what seemed like forever, that I realized I might be in trouble. They were preserving evidence. Against me.

The door was thin, and I could hear a bit of what was

happening outside. Mostly it was a lot of nothing, but while I was waiting, I heard a girl say the words, "Donny Hyslip was with me" followed immediately by a door shutting. She must have been brought into another interview room.

Donny Hyslip was sitting in jail—probably in a cell next to my cousins—accused of killing Reverend Hessel. He didn't do it, I knew that Sue Langtree had done it because she was being blackmailed by the reverend. She'd planted evidence so that Donny would be charged with the murder because he'd raped her granddaughter—plus she wanted to get away with it. Anyway, now it sounded like Donny had an alibi.

Eventually, Lehmann came back. He was a tallish man in his early forties with disappearing beige hair and sad brown eyes. He wore a short-sleeved, plaid shirt that needed ironing. He was either single or had a wife who had little interest in him. Either way, he needed to learn to iron his shirts himself.

"Can I go home soon?"

"We need to go over a few things," he took out a pad on which he'd scribbled some questions. "Why were you at the doctor?"

"I think that's covered by patient/doctor confidentiality." As I said that I tried to read the next question upside down. His handwriting made that nearly impossible.

"That's not true. *You* can tell me why you went. It's Dr. Blinski who can't tell me."

"Because he's dead?"

"No. Because..." He shook his head in frustration, then said, "I'm going to be getting a court order for your records. It would be better if you'd just tell me why you were at the doctor." He was starting to tap his pencil aggressively on the pad.

"Well... you remember that I was run off the road by someone trying to kill me and I ended up with a broken nose and a badly sprained ankle?"

"That was when? April? It's been like five months. Why are you still seeing him?"

"It *still* hurts."

He looked at me as though I was lying. And, course, I was. But 'Dr. Blinski was writing me prescriptions for Oxy any time I asked' did not seem like the kind of answer that would make me look less suspicious.

"Walk me through what happened again." He began doodling on the pad.

"Really? This is like the third time. Do you have memory problems?"

"I just want to make sure I understand everything. You had an appointment, a follow-up on your sprained ankle. Did you arrive on time?"

I fidgeted in the chair. The nylon shorts were not what you'd call comfortable. Then I realized fidgeting probably made me look guilty.

"Yes, I arrived on time. I walked into the lobby and Nancy Fisher told me I could go back to his office. So I did."

"Nancy said that after she sent you back, she heard the door open and then she heard the doctor call out, "Help me." When she got to the office, she found the doctor bleeding to death on the floor while you were trying to climb out the window."

"That's not true. The doctor was already dead when I fell on him. I may have grunted or groaned, or I might have cursed when I fell, that's probably what Nancy heard. And I wasn't trying to climb out the window. I was looking at the bloody fingerprints. Which aren't mine by the way."

"Yeah, those aren't fingerprints so much as smudges. Not sure they'll be much help." Lehmann sighed heavily. "See, the problem is, Nancy says no one was in there with the doctor for at least a half an hour. And the coroner says he hadn't been dead very long before we got there."

"Well, if someone went out the window, they could have

come in that way too. Have you checked the outside of the window?"

"I'll ask the questions, okay?"

"You know, I'm the one who fell on a bloody corpse. I think I deserve sympathy not suspicion."

Lehmann bore down so hard on his pencil that the point broke. "So you want me to believe that someone crawled in the window while the doctor was just sitting there at his desk?"

"Maybe he was in the bathroom."

"Nancy says she would have heard the flush."

"Have you checked her hearing?"

"Her hearing is fine."

"Maybe he didn't flush. Did you check the toilet?"

"Once again, I'm the one asking questions."

"Maybe he walked his patient out and someone climbed in the window while he was saying goodbye."

"There was no patient. They'd just taken lunch."

"Maybe Nancy killed him. Did you think of that?"

"You're the one covered in blood. There's not a drop on her."

Well, he did have a point there.

"Can you tell me which drawer the scalpel was in?" he asked.

"I have no—why would I know something—you're trying to trick me. No, I did not go into the doctor's desk for the scalpel."

"So your fingerprints won't be on it?"

"Are there fingerprints on it?" I remembered it lying there covered in blood. Can you get fingerprints from beneath blood?

"No, it was wiped clean," Lehmann said.

"Then why did you—"

"Do you have any medical training?"

"No. I do not."

"But you do know where the carotid artery is, right?"

"Given the location of Dr. Blinski's wound, I'd say it's in the neck. Do I get a prize for answering that one right?"

"You're a person of interest in this murder. You need to take this seriously."

"I'd much rather be an interesting person than a person of interest."

"You think you can joke your way out of everything, don't you?"

"It's worth a try."

"I don't have to tell you not to leave town, do I?"

"That's funny. The sheriff told me I *should* leave town just a couple of months ago. Maybe the two of you should make up your minds."

When I asked for a ride back to my car, he stormed out of the room and slammed the door. I sat there, slightly confused. I'd been warned not to leave town, so I should probably be able to leave their office. My things, my keys, my wallet, my cell phone, were sitting next to me. I picked up the phone and called my frenemy, Opal.

"Hey, I need a ride," I said when she answered.

"I heard you just bought a car."

"Yeah, and now I need a ride to my car."

"How did you get separated from your car?"

"I'm at the sheriff's office."

"What did you do now?"

"What do you mean, what did *I* do *now*? You make it sound like I'm always breaking the law, which by the way I'm not."

Actually, I *was* but not the point.

"So why are you at the sheriff's office?"

"I'm sort of a murder suspect."

She sighed heavily and said, "All right, I'll pick you up."

Before I left the building, I slipped into the men's room and opened up my wallet. Before I'd given him my clothes, Lehmann had left me alone while he'd gone for evidence bags, so I'd been able to move the Valium I'd borrowed from Bev into my wallet. I swallowed two.

Currently, I was at twenty mils a day of Oxy. I cut a 10 in half first thing in the morning, taking one piece then and the other six hours later. Yeah, yeah, yeah... the directions say do not do this, but I kept forgetting to ask Dr. Blinski for 5s. Well, maybe not forgetting. Taking less Oxy seemed wise, having less did not. If you know what I mean.

Anyway, it was mid-afternoon, so I was way beyond the time to take another half. I'd started to feel nauseated; my hands were kind of shaking, my head was starting to ache, and I'd gotten quite sweaty. The Valium would help with all that.

Opal's 'ladybug' pulled up in front of the Municipal Center. It was one of those 'new' Beetles in red. It had black spots stuck on here and there and eyelashes attached to the headlights. Opal never had trouble finding her car in a parking lot. Actually, that was more of an L.A. problem than a Wyandot County one.

Anyway, she pulled up and I hopped in. Opal was around my age, she was slightly chubby, bisexual, and all around annoying. That afternoon I immediately noticed that her close-cropped hair had been dyed in black-and-white squares. You could literally play chess on her head. Well, checkers.

She must have noticed my staring because she said, "What?" in a very belligerent way.

"Um, you know, I've never asked. Where do you get your hair done?"

"I have to drive down to Grand Rapids."

That made sense. I couldn't imagine that anyone in a two-hundred-mile radius had the skills, or inclination, to do that to a person's head.

"You like it?" she asked.

"It's definitely attention getting," I said.

Fine, I'll admit it. I thought it was kind of cool. But I hated the possibility, remote as it was, that anyone in Wyandot County could be as cool as I was. Or cooler? No, not possible.

Before she could ask me any other questions, I added, "My car is on Main Street in Masons Bay."

She turned the ladybug off. "We're not going anywhere until you explain. You're a murder suspect?"

"I may have exaggerated a bit. I'm a person of interest."

"That's another way to say murder suspect."

"Oh. So I didn't exaggerate?"

"No, I don't think so. Who did you kill?"

"No one. All I did was go to the doctor."

"Dr. Blinski is dead?"

"I literally fell on his corpse. Which by the way was painful. But nobody seems to care about that."

"Yeah. Were you coming from the Y?"

"No, these are Detective Lehmann's. It's all they had. They *took* my clothes. And now they're refusing to rinse the blood out, so they're ruined."

"Dr. Blinski was stabbed?"

"In the carotid artery." I mean, Detective Lehmann had just used the correct term and my short-term memory was excellent for a little while.

"Don't be an asshole. Speak English."

"He was stabbed in the neck."

"Ick. I feel nauseous."

"And you didn't slide around in his blood."

"Oh God, that is so disgusting!"

"Can we go get my car now?"

"Why did you kill Dr. Blinski?"

"I didn't. I think I mentioned that." The Valiums had begun to kick in. I wasn't as nauseous, and the sweating seemed to stop. And the headache faded.

"So why do they think you killed him?"

"His nurse says she heard me kill him and when she came

into the room I was covered in blood and trying to climb out the window."

"That sounds easy to explain," she said sarcastically.

"Actually, it is. I walked into the room and fell onto the corpse. I grunted or groaned or I might have even have said, 'Fuck me'—it would not have been out of character—and then I got up and noticed bloody fingerprints on the windowsill. I was looking at them when Nancy came into the room and started screaming bloody murder. Literally."

"You're in a shitload of trouble, aren't you?" She started the ladybug and we drove away.

"So, what do they think your motive is for killing Dr. Blinski?"

"I don't think they know."

"Depraved drug addict."

"I beg your pardon?"

"Everyone knows that Dr. Blinski was running a pill mill."

"They did?"

"And everyone knows you have a drug problem."

"They do?"

"So you just put two and two together and you get—"

"Seven."

"No, four."

"No, seven. If I'm a depraved drug addict, and I'm not saying I am, but if I was, why would I kill my supplier? Wouldn't that be awfully dumb?"

She opened her mouth to speak, but I interrupted her. "And don't say everyone knows I'm a moron."

"I was going to say you might be right. I mean, you hear about crimes that are drug deals gone wrong all the time—well, at least on TV. But if you think about it, a drug deal is easy. Here's the cash, here's the drugs. Pretty simple, right? The only time it's a drug deal gone wrong is when one person decides to steal from the other person."

"But there's nothing to steal from Dr. Blinski. He's just

giving you a prescription. I guess he could take your seventy-five bucks and not give you anything, but then you'd never go back so it's hard to imagine him doing that."

"Yeah. Why give up the future revenue?" Opal said, as we turned off Duck Pond Road onto Main Street. A few seconds later we pulled up next to my car.

"Is that blue thing your car? I hope you bought more life insurance."

"There's nothing wrong with my car."

"Unless you actually want to get somewhere."

"You have no room to talk."

"Lydia," she began—and yes, she'd named her car. "Lydia, is very reliable."

"Who needs reliability when you can have a convertible?"

"You live in Michigan. We have these very common weather events called snow, rain, ice, gusting wind and frigid cold. You're going to have to put the top up soon and leave it there for about nine months."

"It's almost eighty degrees out."

"And tomorrow it'll be fifty. Wait and see."

"Whatever," I said, getting out of the car. I didn't even bother to say goodbye or thanks for the ride. I wanted to flip her off but settled for sticking out my tongue. When she drove off, I think she was laughing.

As I was about to get into my car, I looked over at Dr. Blinski's office. There was a bit of yellow caution tape across the front door, but that was it. Really, you'd have no idea someone was murdered there just five hours ago. I rashly decided there was something I wanted to see before I drove home.

I say rashly, because I didn't expect anyone to offer a reward, nor did I think my grandmother would pay me, so I had no reason to stick my nose into this murder. Yeah, I was a person of interest, but I didn't expect that to last long. Detective Lehmann would realize that he didn't have any actual evidence and start trying to find the real killer. Meanwhile, I would be minding my own business. Well, I'd be minding my own business right after I took a look underneath the window I was supposedly trying to crawl out of.

The window faced north, I think, or at least it was on the left side of the house as you faced it. On that side of the house was another converted house, this one for a lawyer's office on the first floor and an accountant on the second. It was about twenty feet away with a wide hedge separating the houses. I walked across the lawn and was standing under the window in just a few moments. The side of the house was clapboards painted white and the window was about five feet off the ground. Just low enough that I could look in if I stood on my tippy toes.

There was a large rust-colored stain on the sill and just below on the wall of the house. The killer, covered in blood, had rubbed up against the house as they climbed out. Before I got too close to the window, I looked over the ground. It was badly in need of landscaping. There were patches of dirt and weedy plants here and there.

Directly beneath the window there was a dirt patch with a very clear footprint in it. There was no indication they'd taken a plaster casting. Which was a shame. If this was *CSI*, they'd have done that immediately and then, using nothing but the casting, extrapolated the height of the killer, the brand of sneaker as determined by the tread pattern, traced it back to where and when it had been sold and solved the murder based on a credit card slip.

Leaning against the building, I carefully compared my own foot to the footprint. It was bigger. By quite a bit. My shoe size was nine and a half. Whoever had stood there was probably a size twelve. Of course, it wasn't a sneaker. It was a shoe with a flat sole that gave very little information. Still, they should have taken a mold.

I took out my brand-new Samsung A600 cell phone, which also took pictures. After I bought my car, I'd driven over to the Traverse City Mall to the Verizon Wireless store and upgraded my cell phone. Since it was my mother's plan, she was due for an unpleasant surprise. Hopefully, she wasn't planning to get out of that contract any time in the next decade. The lighting was terrible since the sun was on its way down, but the dark, grainy photo was better than nothing.

Plus, I could put it in sepia tone if I wanted it to look cool.

CHAPTER THREE

I had to drive through Masons Bay to get to my Nana Cole's house which was about a ten-minute drive to the opposite side of the village. Her farm was around thirty-five acres but was not what you'd call a working farm. It was on West Shore Road and had two cherry orchards in the front, which her neighbor farmed and gave her half the profits.

In most years she kept a large thriving kitchen garden. That didn't happen this year since her stroke prevented her from gardening and I had about as much interest in gardening as I did in joining the Marines. Actually, the Marines was more appealing since it would include showering with athletic young men.

Reilly saw me and came running, ears flapping. When he reached me, he let me pet his head but I couldn't say his interest was out of affection. It was dinner time, after all. Once in the kitchen, I grabbed his bowl filled it halfway with kibble then plunked a half a can of wet food on top of it. I put the disgusting mess on the floor and he very nearly swallowed it in one gulp.

Nana Cole was in the living room watching *9&10 News*. When I walked into the room, she picked up the remote and started hitting buttons, changing the channel, raising the volume, turning on the menu. I took it from her and hit the mute button.

"Why on earth did you kill Dr. Blinski?"

"Seriously? That's how much confidence you have in me? I did *not* kill Dr. Blinski."

"That's not what people are saying."

"You're going to believe your friends over me?"

She side-stepped the question and said, "Nancy is telling people she saw you kill the doctor."

"She'd better not be telling people that. She told the sheriff she *heard* me kill him."

"So, you did kill him."

"She heard wrong."

"Where did you get those clothes?"

"They belong to Detective Lehmann. He had to take my clothes as evidence, so he gave me these—"

"Why are your clothes evidence?"

"They're covered in blood."

"Your clothes are covered in blood, but you didn't kill Dr. Blinski?"

"I fell on him *after* he was dead."

"Oh my God... that's..." She recoiled in horror. "Why would you tell me something like that?"

"Because you keep calling me a murderer."

"Don't be so offended. You wouldn't be the first murderer in the family."

I don't know why she thought that was comforting.

I said, "I'm going upstairs to take a shower. Then I'm going to have dinner."

"There's meatloaf."

"Yum."

Before I could leave the room, she asked, "What is it with you? Always getting involved with murder."

"Me? What is it with you? Your cousin. Your minister. Your doctor. It's like you're a murder magnet."

"There's no such thing."

"If there were such a thing you would be it."

I turned and left the room. She called after me, "I'm not paying you to find out who killed Dr. Blinski. I don't care."

I suspected she did care. At least a little. He was her doctor, after all, and now she had to find a new one. Of course, so did I. And that was a problem... one I'd think about later.

It was a thrill to take a shower. Detective Lehmann had taken me into the men's room for photographs while I was still dressed. He wanted to get a sense of where there was blood both on and off my clothing. He'd watched me take my clothes off and put them into evidence bags, then taken pictures of me mostly naked. I thought that was kind of pervy. And not in the good way.

After that, he left me alone to get dressed. I was able to take a whore's bath in the sink but not much more. I'd had the feeling of being covered in blood for hours. I don't recommend it.

Washing my hair, I started thinking about the scalpel. It meant something. Maybe several somethings. Did it mean that whoever killed Dr. Blinski hadn't planned to? Had they realized they needed to kill him and just grabbed whatever was available? Maybe.

That was one something.

Another something: Had Dr. Blinski left the scalpel on his desk and the person just grabbed it? Or was it in a drawer, meaning that the killer knew just where to find it?

A very important something.

And here's another something: Why did Dr. Blinski even have a scalpel? He was your basic country doctor. But wait, that meant he did everything. Like lancing boils and cutting off gross moles, and removing little cysts just below—okay, there were lots of reasons he had a scalpel. So, why didn't the killer take it with them?

That might not be too hard to answer. Personally, I'd find it a challenge to climb through a window with a scalpel in my pocket without requiring stiches. But did this person think that quickly? I mean, it had taken hours for me to think of it.

Ah—shampoo in my eyes. Eek.

After I thoroughly rinsed the shampoo out of my eyes and stopped the intense pain, I got out of the shower and toweled off. When I got upstairs, I went into my mother's old bedroom. My bedroom. The TV downstairs was very loud and I could hear the *Big Brother* music. I'd managed to hook my Nana Cole on the very trashy show. It was one of the few things we agreed on. Hating spoiled, straight, White twentysomethings.

In the bedroom, I took out my stash, which I kept in a pair of dress shoes I had little call for. I had five and a half 10s left. I was way overdue for my half 10, so I took that quickly and started to calculate how long five 10s would last. It was ten doses, so I had enough for two and a half days. I might be able to stretch it to three.

Reilly came into the room and stood next to me until I petted his head. As I scratched his ears, I realized I was going to be in trouble soon. Very real trouble.

***

THE NEXT MORNING, I woke up very late. *Very*. I'd stayed up until two playing *World of Warcraft III*. My eyes flew open when the Stars and Stripes ringtone on my phone went off. I'd chosen that one for Vinnie because it was loud and obnoxious, just like him.

Still, we'd been on the outs so I was thrilled he was calling me. "Hello!" I said, happily.

He replied with, "Moochie! He left me!"

"Carlos?"

"Of course, Carlos. For God's sake, how many boyfriends do you think I have?"

"Okay, I'm sorry he left you. You must be—"

"Heartbroken. I *am*. I wish it wasn't such a long drive to the ocean. I'd throw myself into the surf like James Mason in *A Star Is Born*."

"You could try rolling your car in the desert like Kris Kristofferson in *A Star Is Born*."

"The desert? Are you serious? With my complexion?" Then he gasped and said, "My life is over."

"Your life isn't over, Vinnie. You'll be fine."

"How would you know? You've never had a serious relationship."

Ouch. I said, "I'm trying to be sympathetic, but that was mean."

"Being mean makes me feel better."

"Um... okay? Continue. If you have to."

"This is all your fault, Moochie. Carlos would never have moved in if you hadn't left. And if he'd never moved in, I'd never have fallen for him. And my heart wouldn't be shattered into a million pieces."

"Um... I'm sorry? Would it make you feel better if I told you a lot of people think I'm a murderer?"

"Oh my God. I can't believe it. It always has to be about you, doesn't it?"

"Not always, no. In fact, I'd really rather not talk about this if you don't mind."

"But you just brought it up, so it seems you do want to talk about it. So go ahead. Tell me all about being a murderer. Is it everything you hoped it would be?"

"I'm not actually a murderer, people just think I am."

"Is that like people just thinking you're a drug addict?"

"No, I actually am—" Oh my God, he tried to trick me into saying I'm a drug addict. How dare he! "I think we should change the subject. I bought a car!"

"You bought a car?"

"It's a convertible."

"You bought a car before you paid me back?"

"I owe you twenty-five bucks; I figured I could give it to you when I see you."

"You owe me twenty-five bucks ten times. Two hundred and fifty dollars. Not to mention a month's rent. For a total of eight hundred fifty dollars."

Why was everyone in my life running a tab on me? It seemed awfully unfair.

"Wait a minute. My mother's boyfriend paid the rent."

"The check bounced. Twice."

"Really? Okay, that's not my fault."

"I didn't say it was your fault. I said you still owe me the money."

"I'll talk to my mother." A chill very nearly ran up my spine. I did not want to talk to her, which Vinnie knew so he really should have said, 'It's fine don't worry about it,' but he didn't. Instead, he said, "I'm going to need a money order this time."

"Sure. I get it. So, you're looking for a new roommate?"

"No, Carlos hasn't moved out. He left *me*, not the apartment."

"You have to live with your ex? That's not going to be fun."

"Darling, tell me about it. He's already talking about moving his boyfriend in."

"He already has a new boyfriend?"

"Well, maybe not *that* new."

"He always had a boyfriend?"

"Every couple has their issues." He inhaled deeply and then said, "Moochie, you have to come back. I think I need to move out and I'm going to need a roommate."

Outside, I heard a couple of cars coming down the driveway. Then my Nana Cole called up the stairs, "Henry, the police are here."

"Vinnie, I have to go. The police are here."

"Oh Moochie. Call me later and let me know if you're in prison."

I clicked off and jumped out of bed. I stripped off my SpongeBob PJs and pulled on a pair of jeans and my favorite T-shirt, the one that had drawings of fish riding on skateboards. Then I slipped on my dress shoes, the ones that had my stash in the toe. Well, they were unlikely to strip search me.

When I opened the bedroom door, Detective Lehmann and a sheriff's deputy were coming up the stairs. Reilly was barking at them. Good boy.

"We need to search your room," Lehmann said.

"Okay. It's a little messy. Maybe you could straighten things up while you're searching."

"That would be a no," he said before entering my room.

I went downstairs, trying to remember if there was anything they could find that was illegal. Anything not already in my shoe, that is. I was coming up with a blank. Though, to be honest, I did sometimes forget where I'd put an Oxy or two. I was, on occasion, delightfully surprised by the return of a pill.

So, they *might* find something. Shouldn't really be a problem though, I was getting them from a doctor, so, while perhaps over prescribed, it wasn't exactly illegal. Was it?

In the living room, Sheriff Dill Crocker stood in front of the television chatting with my Nana Cole. He was in his late-fifties, tall, and thin—with the exception of a round belly straining at his black uniform.

My dog was still barking. I said, "Shhhhh." And surprisingly, he shut up.

The sheriff was saying, "Every family has a black sheep, Emma. And I've arrested most of them."

"The thing about sheep, Dill, is that they're not predators.

Unless you're one of those men who get all fussy about their lawns, they aren't going to do you any harm."

"Just trying to be sympathetic, Emma. Might not have chosen the right words."

"So what are you looking for?" I asked. "You have the murder weapon; you have the clothes I was wearing."

"We're looking for motive. When we find out why you killed the doctor, we'll be arresting you."

"Does that mean you're looking for a note pad that says 'I killed Dr. Blinski, because...'"

"Henry, you're not doing yourself any favors," Nana Cole said.

"Do you have a note pad like that?" Sheriff Crocker asked.

"Of course, not. I have no reason to kill Dr. Blinski."

Actually, it was just the opposite. I had every reason to want him to live. I needed him around until I finished titrating down from my very tiny, itsy bitsy, opioid addiction. This was all really bad. I needed more Oxy and my deal—I mean, doctor—was dead.

"We'll see about that," the sheriff said smugly.

Just then the deputy came down the stairs with my laptop in a large plastic bag.

"Hold on, you can't take that."

"Yes, we can," the sheriff said. Holding out a folded piece of blue paper. "Says so in the search warrant. Computer, cell phone, any and all appointment books, calendars, diaries whether on paper or electronic."

"You can't take my cell phone. I need that."

"You may not need it as much as you think."

What did *that* mean? Oh, wait, he meant I'd be in prison. Apparently, you can't have a cell phone in prison. Well, that had to be unconstitutional.

CHAPTER FOUR

I was back in that awful interview room at the Municipal Center. I mean, it wasn't an awful room for any reason other than the things that went on in there. The walls were nicely paneled in a fake maple. The chair I was given wasn't even uncomfortable. No, the awful part was the sheriff and Detective Lehmann sitting on the other side of the table.

They'd brought me over some time in the midafternoon after they'd gotten bored searching my grandmother's house. I don't think they found anything, which didn't mean they didn't take a lot of things. I guess they planned to spend a lot of time staring at my stuff wondering why it didn't incriminate me.

They left me alone in the room for about an hour, then Sheriff Crocker and Detective Lehmann came in. Before they even sat down, Crocker started yelling at me to confess. I let him go on for a little while before asking, "Does this ever work for you?"

Crocker looked like his head might explode, so Detective Lehmann stepped in. "We'd like to get a palm print from you. It's voluntary. For now."

"Why?" I asked.

"This morning we found a palm print outside Dr. Blinski's window."

"Oh. That's probably mine. When I picked up my car, I took a peek outside Dr. Blinski's window. On the ground beneath the window there was a footprint. I leaned against the house—with my hand, I guess—so I could check the shoe size against my foot. You're looking for a killer with a size eleven and a half or twelve shoe. I took a photo. It's on my cell phone. Which you need to give back."

Detective Lehmann was blushing as red as a stop sign. "That's probably my footprint. I checked the windowsill for prints yesterday."

"So, before you did that, did you look at the ground to see—"

"I don't believe you for one friggin second," Sheriff Crocker said. "You were there, two or three days ago, casing Dr. Blinski's office, weren't you?"

"Why would I do that? I've seen Dr. Blinski, like. a lot. I know where everything is."

"So, you admit to planning the murder."

"No, I do not."

Detective Lehmann shook his head. "We're going through your computer right now. You seem to like pornography."

"I have an appreciation for the male form."

"Some of those models are underage and we're going to prove it," the sheriff yelled before adding, "Disgusting."

Now it was my turn to blush. "I, um, I tend to like hairy guys just a little older than me. You're probably wasting—you know what, whatever floats your boat."

"What about these nasty chat places?" The sheriff asked in the most accusatory way possible.

Oh my God, that was going to be more embarrassing than the porn. Sheriff Crocker got up and opened the door. "Wilcox, get in here. No, bring the laptop with you."

A moment later, Deputy Wilcox walked into the interview

room. He was the same deputy who'd searched my home. He was near my age and looked sheepish and deeply embarrassed. This was probably the worst day he'd had working for the sheriff's department ever. He set my iBook on the table while the sheriff said to me, "Tell us about OpenDoor1975. You know him, right?"

"I wouldn't say I know him. I had a chat with him once. Probably in February or March. That's not actually knowing someone. I don't know his real name for instance."

"Don't worry, we're going to find out his name. But I think I already know it."

Detective Lehmann was being very quiet. I got the feeling he thought this line of questioning just as weird as I did.

"You've been seeing Dr. Blinski quite a lot," Sheriff Crocker said.

"Yes. I told you. My ankle isn't healing right."

I really should remember to limp, I thought.

"Read that line from the chat with OpenDoor1975," he told the deputy.

"From two to four, the lights will be off, the door will be unlocked. You can come in and... and..."

"I remember the chat. You don't have to offend your delicate straight boy sensibilities," I said. "What does this have to do with Dr. Blinski's death?"

"We know he's OpenDoor1975. You've been going to his office to have sex with him!"

"Ew, ick. He's really old. And he has hair in his ears."

"What does that matter? It's dark."

"Hey, maybe you would do him, but I only have sex in the dark with attractive people."

Before the sheriff had a chance to throttle me, Detective Lehmann asked, "So you've never met OpenDoor1975?"

"No. If you continue the chat you can see that I asked him to send me a pic. He wouldn't so I ended the chat. And... you do know that when people put a date in their screen name it's typically their birth year."

"1975 is the year Dr. Blinski married his first wife," the sheriff said.

"Yeah, not the same."

He got very close to my face and said, "You're too calm. Only someone guilty is that calm."

"That doesn't make any sense. I'm calm because I know I didn't kill Dr. Blinski."

Of course, dipping into my stash when they gave me a bathroom break didn't hurt.

"Innocent people are always nervous."

"Because you put innocent people in jail?"

"You bet your ass—wait, no that's not right—"

Detective Lehmann stepped in and said as definitively as possible, "We do *not* put innocent people in jail."

"So I have no reason to be nervous, do I?"

Lehmann stood up and said, "Sheriff, can you step outside with me?"

Moments later, they stood right outside the interview room arguing. I could hear most of what they were saying. Sheriff Crocker wanted to arrest me right then, but Detective Lehmann pointed out they didn't have enough evidence. The sheriff actually used the phrase "Evidence be damned!" before they walked away from the door.

As I waited, I wondered if maybe I should be more worried. Innocent people did go to prison, sometimes on less evidence than they had on me.

What evidence was there, though? A couple of bloody, smudgy fingerprints on the windowsill. Given that we can't establish that anyone was there but Nancy Fisher and me, the killer had to have entered and left through the window. The fingerprints and the fact that Dr. Blinski's carotid artery was severed meant that the killer was covered in blood when they left. Which was confirmed by the large rust-colored stain on the outside of the window.

It was the middle of the day, so they must have had a car nearby. Probably in the back alley. I wondered if they'd even bothered to ask around if anyone saw anything. Or had they been too busy searching my bedroom.

Detective Lehmann came back into the room with an ink pad and a large fingerprint card. He was alone. He put a consent form in front of me and asked me to sign it. I did. I mean, I knew they weren't my fingerprints. Well, the one's on the windowsill.

As he inked my fingers and rolled them on the card, I asked, "You don't really think I did it, do you?"

He sighed heavily. "I've done a little bit of research on blood. The blood we found on your clothes and body; those bloodstains were blotchy, thick. Consistent with falling into a puddle of blood. If you'd killed him, you'd have been standing and you would have been covered in what's called arterial spray. That's a different kind of pattern. We found arterial spray on the walls, the exam table, the desk... but not on you."

"So, I'm in the clear?"

"Not really. Crocker thinks you might have deliberately rubbed yourself on the body after he stopped bleeding so much. I don't think you're that smart."

I could be that smart. Blood spatter might have been covered on *CSI*. I couldn't remember at that particular moment if I'd seen an episode where they did that. But I might have. I decided I really shouldn't tell him that.

"What about the blood stain outside?"

"The sheriff thinks you killed Blinski, climbed out the window and then changed your mind and climbed back in."

"Why would I change my mind?"

"You realized that if you disappeared, you'd be the only suspect."

Oh God, that almost made sense. Now he was inking up

my palm and pressing it to the card. Lord knows why, I'd already told them that was my palm print.

"We're going to need to get a blood spatter expert to talk to us. Pricey. And time consuming."

He handed me a packet of Wet-Wipes to get the ink off my hands. I said, "The killer must have had a car nearby. Probably in the back."

"I've got a deputy over there now talking to the neighbors."

"So, I *am* in the clear?"

"The sheriff wants it to be you. The thing is, if we arrest you and go to trial, your attorney will want to know what other leads were followed. That's how I'm getting him to hold off and investigate things not related to you."

"Isn't there a camera in here?" I asked. He couldn't want the sheriff to hear this conversation.

"I turned it off when I came back in."

That was a good thing. That meant there *was* video of the sheriff screaming at me to confess. That might be useful if they did arrest me.

Detective Lehmann stood up and said, "You're free to go."

"Um... do I get a phone call?"

"You get a phone call if we arrest you. We haven't arrested you."

"Yeah, but you have my cell phone. And you drove me here."

He sighed heavily—he seemed to be good at that—and said, "All right. Come to my office."

BIG PROBLEM. Opal's number was in my phone and I didn't remember it. I couldn't call information because they didn't give out cell phone numbers. And, also, I didn't remember Opal's last name; or if I ever asked for it. So I asked

Detective Lehmann, "There's a boutique in Masons Bay. Opal works there..."

He said, "I don't know everybody who works in the village."

"She's the girl always changing her hair color. She was involved with the reward—"

"Pastiche," he said.

"Thanks."

I called information, wrote down the number on a pad and made the call.

"This is Pastiche," Opal said.

"Thank God. Can you come and get me?"

"Henry?"

"Of course, it's Henry."

"Where are you?"

"I'm at the sheriff's office. Again."

"Can you wait three hours?"

"No."

"Okay, I get a break so I'll just put a sign on the door that I'll be back in fifteen minutes. You'll have to hang out here. I can't drive you home until we close, that would take too long."

"Okay," I said. I mean, it was better than waiting at the sheriff's office for three hours. Wasn't it?

"Wait outside," she said, and then hung up.

She picked me up in Lydia the ladybug about five minutes later, barely stopping to let me into the car. We were back on Duck Pond Road in seconds.

"Who did you kill now?" she asked.

"No one. They're still trying to pin Dr. Blinski's murder on me. Mainly, the sheriff hates me and wants to put me in prison for any reason."

"Lucky you. You should call your grandmother when we get to the store. She'll be worried."

"She's fine. She doesn't need to know my every move." I had a million questions I wanted to ask Opal that might help get me out of trouble, but I figured I'd better at least pretend to care about her, so I asked, "How are *you*?"

"Given that no one's accused me of murder recently, great."

"Is Pastiche busy?"

"Actually, yes. This is the last big week of summer. Fall officially starts next week."

We parked in front of the store. The movie theater was playing the new *Freaky Friday* movie and the fudge store was having a sale, fifty percent off your second pound. Pastiche was squeezed in between.

Opal unlocked the door and we went inside. The place had a very particular vibe. Pretty much everything in the store looked like a large shawl, whether it was or not. Brown and orange were favorite colors. Opal's outfit, which I suspected she only wore at the store, was decades too old for her.

She sat down on a stool behind the cash register, and said, "Make yourself comfortable."

That was going to be difficult.

"So, tell me everything you know about Dr. Blinski," I said.

"Well, you've probably figured out there are a lot of Polish people up here. He's from one of those families. Second generation maybe, I don't know. I heard he came back here after medical school and married his high school sweetheart."

"She must be devastated."

"Maybe not. She lives in Florida with her second husband. After the divorce he married his nurse."

"Nancy Fisher?"

"No. The one before Nancy."

"She must be devastated," I repeated.

"Well, sure. Someone murdered her meal ticket."

"Do you know her name?"

"Helena Blinski. She comes in all the time. She'll probably be in this weekend to buy something black."

"When do you think the funeral will be?"

"Probably not until later next week. I mean, Monday feels too soon. So does Tuesday. Probably not until Friday."

"Are there kids?"

"Yeah, a bunch."

"How many are a bunch?"

"Five, I think."

"What are their names?"

"Blinski."

"I meant their first names."

"I'm not entirely sure. You could check the phone book. Anyone named Blinski is probably one of his relatives."

"There are other doctors up here, aren't there?"

"Of course, there are. But none like Dr. Blinski, if that's what you're asking. At least not that I know about."

Well, that was a bummer. It was clear that what she meant by 'none like Dr. Blinski' was that there weren't other doctors willing to prescribe Oxy without actual evidence of injury. That meant I was in a lot of trouble.

Then I had an unusual thought. One of the pitfalls of enjoying recreational drugs is going a little too far and ending up dead. Obviously, that would never happen to me. I mean, I suppose it almost happened once but, seriously, it would *never* happen again.

It did happen to other people, though. It was possible that Dr. Blinski gave out too many pills to someone and they died. Which might have made someone else angry, angry enough to climb through his window and kill him.

Yeah, probably not. If I *had* overdosed, I could not imagine my grandmother being angry enough to kill someone. I doubted she'd be all that sad. Which in itself was sad, wasn't it?

CHAPTER FIVE

Opal was in a rush when she dropped me off at Nana Cole's farm. Apparently, on Saturday nights she poured cider at Tip Top Tap. That made no sense. She was a girl with a trust fund. If I had a trust fund you wouldn't find me working one job, no less two. I'd be on a beach, like Santa Monica Beach or Laguna Beach. Or any beach.

Reilly was waiting at the backdoor for me. I didn't even have to call him. There was a tennis ball nearby. I picked it up and threw it. Sometimes he'd chase after it. And sometimes he'd just stare at me with this look that said, "Humans are so weird." Today was definitely the latter.

"Fine, don't chase it," I said before we went into the kitchen to find Nana Cole cooking. Reilly ran across the room, sniffed his empty bowl, and then ran down the hallway heading upstairs to lay on my bed.

Since her stroke, Nana cooking was always a suspenseful event. She'd used a walker for the first few months and then finally moved to a cane. That was as much progress as she'd made. She'd have made more progress if she'd stuck with physical therapy, but that didn't happen. I was angry at her about that for a while. But then I remembered how annoying she was when she *could* get around.

At some point, she'd knocked over one of the kitchen chairs. I picked it up, set it right, then asked, "What are you making?"

"I've roasted a chicken; I'm making mashed potatoes and green beans. I'm starting some gravy and I'm going to whip up some biscuits in a minute."

She leaned back and wobbled on her cane. I tried not to gasp. She'd very nearly pitched herself onto the stove.

"That's a lot of food. You must have been pretty confident they'd let me go."

"Not really. Bev is coming over."

"Oh."

"When you're done with that set the table for three," Nana Cole said.

As I set the table, I decided I wouldn't volunteer any information unless she asked. I laid out all the plates. The silverware. The glasses. And folded the napkins so they looked fancy on the plates. Not a peep from Nana Cole. I said, "Well, I'm going upstairs. I have a phone call to make."

"Aren't you going to tell me what happened at with the sheriff?"

"Oh, I wasn't sure you were interested."

She turned and glared at me until I coughed up the info. "Well, Sheriff Croker thinks I did it and no amount of evidence to the contrary will convince him."

"In school, I was friends with his older sister. He was always a stubborn little brat. Not very bright either."

"Really? Didn't you vote for him to be sheriff?"

"Three times."

"You don't see the problem there?"

"You didn't see the other candidates."

She walked over to the pantry to get the flour. She walked

like a penguin, one who might wallop you with their walking stick at any moment.

"They didn't have enough evidence to keep you then?"

"They don't have *any* evidence."

"That's not what people are saying."

"Is that what you did while I was gone? Gossip about me?"

"I thought you'd want to know."

Okay, maybe I did, a little. I mean, if this was my fifteen minutes of fame, so be it.

"Well... what are they saying?"

"Jan thinks you were trying to steal from him."

"They keep the money in Nancy Fisher's desk. I know that you know that. Everyone knows that. When you pay, Nancy puts it in her drawer. If I wanted to rob them, I'd have killed Nancy and taken the money."

"That's true. I'll tell Jan. Oh, and she also told me that Donny Hyslip's girlfriend, Angela something, told the sheriff she was with Donny the night of Reverend Hessel's murder."

"Do people believe her?"

"No, no one does."

"Okay, I'm going to make that phone call now," I said.

But as I left the room—

"Dorothy thinks the doctor was your father."

"Excuse me?! He's my father so I killed him?"

"She also thinks he raped your mother which is why she won't tell anyone who your father is."

"She won't tell anyone who my father is because she can't remember his name. And that all happened out in California. You did tell her she was wrong, didn't you?"

"Well, you know how people are when you contradict them."

"Didn't any of your friends think I was being falsely accused?"

"Now that you mention it, no."

"Did you even suggest the possibility?"

"It was a fact-finding mission. I wasn't there to win hearts and minds." She watched Fox News too much, which is why she often sounded like Dick Cheney defending the Iraq War regardless of the subject.

"I'm going upstairs."

"Tell your mother I said hello," she called after me. *How did she know?* I wondered. Probably the gloomy look of dread on my face.

Upstairs, I took my shoe off and retrieved my stash. I took my half 10 a little early. I mean, I couldn't pop it in the middle of dinner. Then I unplugged the DSL and plugged in my mother's ancient pink princess phone, which was usually in the closet. I dialed the number, thinking rotary phones are so weird. How do they even work?

"Hello, Henry, how are you?" she said, after I said "Hey."

Ignoring that, I cut to the chase. "I spoke to Vinnie. He said the check you gave him for the rent bounced. Twice."

"And you're angry. That's so sweet of you to stick up for your friend. But remember, I'm your mother."

"You need to get him a money order. We're talking about February's rent. It's September."

"Exactly. It's been a long time. I'm sure he's gotten over it. I mean, does he even need the money?"

"He's a barista."

"He's working for tips? That means he's rolling in cash."

"It's a crime to write bad checks."

"Oh... you think no one has ever tried that one on me? Go ahead, threaten your mother with jail."

"It's not even your money. David paid him. Why are David's checks bouncing?"

"You don't know anything about rich people. They always have cash flow problems."

"If rich people are always broke then why are they rich people?"

"Because they have assets." Then, she said, "Look, why don't you just pay your friend yourself?"

"Because I'm broke. Which apparently means I'm rich."

"Oh no dear, you don't have any assets." Before I could ask her to pay the debt again, she wondered, "Is this the only reason you called me? You don't care at all how I am?"

That was a tough question. I kind of didn't. Or at least didn't want to. Still, I asked, "How are you?"

"Amazing. I've really taken to life at sea."

I resisted saying something about her always being adrift.

"The sunrises and the sunsets, they're just amazing. And the dolphins! We see packs of them all the time. It's one of the most moving experiences of my life."

"Mmmm-hmmm."

"Oh darling, can't you be happy for me?"

"Let's make a deal, you pay Vinnie and I'll be happy for you living on a yacht."

"Ugh, it's a boat," she said, and then clicked off.

DINNER WAS EXCRUCIATING. Nana Cole and Bev talked about how the president was coming to Michigan—somewhere down by Detroit, which might as well be on the moon as far as I was concerned—and they talked about their friend Barbara whose grandson Josh had died in Iraq. Bev had been spending a lot of time with her. Apparently, the town of Masons Bay wanted to make a big deal about Josh when Veteran's Day rolled around in November. Barbara wasn't having it and had managed to anger a lot of people in the process, my Nana Cole included.

"People are just trying to be nice."

"That's not an excuse to ignore Barbara's feelings, Emma."

"But she should be proud. Josh was fighting for our freedom."

"On the other side of the world. It's kind of a stretch."

"Whoever you've been listening to is telling you lies."

"The whole reason we went into Afghanistan was to find Osama Bin Laden. And we haven't done that."

"And that's why we're still there."

"Are we even looking for him? If we find him, we'll have to leave."

"You really don't know what you're talking about."

"I probably don't, Emma. But I am willing to listen. Don't you think you should start listening?"

That didn't go over well. They haggled back and forth for a while, as I wondered how long I had to sit there before I could say I had to run an errand. That morning, when I was feeding Reilly, I'd noticed we were going to need canned dog food in a few days. Nana Cole wasn't paying much attention to my dog, so it would be easy enough to say I had to go and buy him some food before we ran out.

Which is what I did.

"Can't you go in the morning?" Nana Cole asked.

"I think it's supposed to rain tomorrow."

"It is," Bev confirmed.

Of course, there was no reason I couldn't drive in the rain, but I was out the door before Nana Cole could mention that. I decided not to put the top up just yet. As Opal said, once it goes up it will probably stay there for months on end. I decided to enjoy it, even though temperature had abruptly dropped into the low sixties.

I drove out Turtle Highway toward Coldwater. Quickly, I realized I was not going to be able to keep the top down. Despite the fact that my car was basically unable to break the speed limit, the wind still brought the temperature down twenty degrees. I pulled over into someone's driveway and spent ten minutes struggling to get the top up. There was a large plastic panel that you had to remove in order to get the convertible top to come out. Once you did that, it didn't really go back on, instead it floated around in the back seat. Anyway, I finally got it attached and continued my trip.

I arrived at Queens Way Mobile Home Park about twenty minutes later only to discover there was nowhere to park. The trailer park was very small, just one road with mobile homes on either side. Ronnie Sheck lived in number fifteen which was right at the front. I drove by twice before I realized he was the reason there was nowhere to park. There was a line of people waiting to get into his trailer. I almost gave up, but realized what a bad idea that was.

I parked and then walked back down the street. I got in line outside number fifteen. Central casting would have been very disappointed in the people standing outside Ronnie Sheck's. They looked like normal people. Middle-aged house-wives, construction workers, honor students, two guys in MSU football jerseys. I got in line behind a senior citizen smoking an extra-long cigarette, who had bright tangerine hair and a well-engineered push-up bra.

The most interesting thing about the ten or twelve people who stood outside of Ronnie Sheck's trailer was that—to me, at least—they looked exactly like the kind of people who would vote for anti-crime, let's-win-the-war-on-drugs, candidates. I doubted any of them would support a candidate who said we should legalize drugs. I would though, which I guess made me the oddball.

I asked the neon-haired woman in front of me, "Are you a patient of Dr. Blinski's?"

"I was, yes. I had an appointment at four thirty on Friday. I've been kind of panicky ever since."

"Because you don't have any pills?"

"Well, that too... Mostly I'm afraid of someone trying to stick a scalpel in my throat. I mean, why him? He did so much good in the world."

Someone came out of the trailer. A middle-aged guy in stained clothes that didn't fit. He needed a haircut, a shave, and about a week at a health spa. The kind of place that featured sandblasting.

"You get what you needed?" someone asked him.

"Some," he said. "He doesn't have a lot."

Oh great, I thought.

Randomly, the woman in front of me said, "There's a good doctor down in Cadillac. I've heard you just have to say you have back pain. He doesn't ask where, just writes you a prescription. With refills."

I couldn't help myself, "Do you know his name?"

"I don't. I've just heard."

"Eastman," said the construction guy in front of her. "I called this morning. You can't get an appointment for six weeks."

"Six weeks?" she said. "I can't wait six weeks. Shit."

That was met with a nervous silence. None of us could wait six weeks.

"Is Ronnie the only game in town?" I asked.

"Yes and no. There's a guy over in Elmwood Township and then another in Honor. You've got to have reliable transportation, though. And an introduction."

I wondered for a moment if she was slighting my car. Had she seen it when I drove up?

"I mean, there are other ways," she said. "Lots of people have Oxy they don't want. I know that sounds crazy, but they get these prescriptions and then they don't finish them. Which doesn't make any sense to me. I had this neighbor, used to be some kind of cop. He really wanted to fuck me. I heard he had some kind of surgery, so I'd go over and flirt with him every so often and he'd give me five, ten pills at a time. I never fucked him though. I'm not that kind of girl."

The last part she said as though she was proud of herself. Which was a little weird, but then she added, "He died. Cancer."

"Oh wow, that's sad."

And creepy. She'd cock-teased a cancer patient out of painkillers and was proud of it.

"Yeah. I wish he was still around. I wouldn't be standing here, let me tell you."

I suppose I shouldn't criticize. Allowing a casual leisure activity to become an actual addition is not something to boast about, either. And we won't even talk about the things I've done for drugs. Not that I can remember most of them.

A couple more people went in and came out. I was getting anxious. Not because I needed a pill, but because I needed a bunch of pills. I wasn't ready to completely titrate down and I certainly wasn't ready to go cold turkey. Ronnie Sheck needed to come through for me.

When it was finally my turn to enter the trailer, I went inside. It was pretty much the same as the first time I was there. The living room was wall to wall gross furniture, the place smelled of pot. There were some guys sitting around. I couldn't tell if they were the same guys who were sitting around the last time I came. Two of them might be, one of them was new. He had an eyebrow ring and didn't look quite as baked as the others. Maybe he was here before, I couldn't really be sure.

Sitting with them was Ronnie. He was a short, scrawny guy who looked fifteen but was actually thirty. Now *he* was totally baked. Probably celebrating his good fortune even while he was in the midst of it.

Once he managed to focus on me, he said, "Oh. You. I remember you. Here's the deal. You buy a quarter ounce of pot; I sell you six 10s. That's a hundred bucks. You buy a half an ounce; I sell you twelve 10s. A hundred and seventy-five."

Option B was pretty much every cent I had, but given the conversation I'd had outside I figured I should go for it.

While I was counting out his money, I asked, "Did you know Dr. Blinski?"

"Sure. He was my doctor when I was a kid. I don't

normally deal in pills. I'm only doing this out of respect of his memory."

"That's really sweet of you."

"I know, isn't it?"

One of his lackies handed me my dope and another snatched the money out of my hand. I asked Ronnie, "Can you think of anyone who might want Dr. Blinski dead? I mean, someone dealing... Besides you I mean. I don't think you killed him. Someone else, who might want to take over his business, that's a motive."

Was that true? Ronnie Sheck was probably making a killing. That would be a good motive to kill Dr. Blinski. He tried harder to focus on me. Had I said the wrong thing?

"Sure, there are other doctors like Blinski around here. I don't think any of them would do something to Blinski, though. I mean, the hypocrite oath and all. Besides, there's plenty to go around, you know?"

"What are their names?"

"Like I'm going to tell you that." He started giggling.

"But I'm not sure you're going to have enough to take care of me."

He was still giggling when he said, "Then I guess you're shit out of luck."

CHAPTER SIX

Nothing interesting happened that Sunday. I did not get arrested or brought in for questioning a third time or fall over another body. I did sleep too late to take my grandmother to church—not unplanned—so she had to call her friend Jan to take her, but not without banging around enough to make sure I knew she was angry with me.

It was raining, so after she left I went out and checked on my car. The rip in the convertible top was leaking, so I went back inside and grabbed a towel and a bowl. I pressed the towel into the now damp seat and positioned the bowl so it would catch most of the dripping water. This explained why there was a slight musty smell when I put the top up. I made a mental note that I had to stay a couple of days in Palm Springs on my way home. The desert air would dry out most things. After I fed and walked Reilly, I decided the two of us needed to go back to bed. He was completely amenable. I took a full 10, figuring I'd titrate down tomorrow. Hey, if you were accused of murder, you'd stop cutting your Oxys in half, too.

By Monday morning it had stopped raining, so I tossed out the contents of the bowl I'd left in the backseat before leaving for the Conservancy and spread the towel out on the seat to dry. When I got to the office, Bev handed me a little silver digital camera and told me to go out to Revold Road and check out the Schmidt farm. Rumor had it they were cutting down trees they shouldn't in order to add another field on the part of their farm they'd put under nonagricultural conservancy. She gave me strict instructions to take the pictures from the road and not to engage with the owners. That was more than okay by me.

The sky had cleared and was a pretty blue, but the temperature had dipped down and I'd had to bring a leather bomber jacket I'd gotten at Goodwill. I was also wearing a slick pair of black jeans that I allowed to crumple up on top of my shoes, a black mesh T-shirt on top of a regular yellow one, and a pair of John Lennon sunglasses. My hair was a mess but no one in two counties was fashionable enough to figure that out.

I found a spot on Revold Road that had a good view of the farm. They were definitely taking down trees. I had a site map with me, but it was difficult to tell if they were cutting down trees that were under conservancy or just going right up to the line. From a distance, I started snapping photos.

Behind me I heard tires on gravel and turned to see that a large black SUV pulling up to me. It was a pretty new Lincoln Navigator which, honestly, just looked like a station wagon on steroids. After it stopped, a guy just few years older than I am got out. He had shaggy blond hair and a thin goatee. He gave me a broad smile as he walked over.

"Interesting car. Do you have a death wish?"

He had to be a Schmidt pissed off about my taking photos, and I was definitely not supposed to engage. I opened my car door and was about to get in, when the guy asked, "You're Henry Milch, aren't you?"

"Mooch."

"Did you just burp at me?"

"No, it's my nickname."

"If that was my nickname, I wouldn't tell people."

"Okay, well, I need to go now," I said. I'd already engaged far too much with someone I wasn't supposed to engage with.

"Well, hold on, take my card," he said, holding out a business card.

I took it and read:

Hamlet Gilbody, Jr.
Private Detective
Grand Rapids
616-358-4232

"HAMLET? REALLY?"

"You can call me Ham. See, that's a nickname."

"Why am I calling you anything?"

"Because I'm following you."

I offered him his card back.

"Oh no, keep that. That's why I gave it to you. To keep."

"Why are you following me?" I said, shoving his card into my back pocket where I planned to forget it. Someday I'd find a soggy lump at the bottom of the washing machine and wonder what it was.

"Dr. Blinski's family, they want me to prove you killed him. Casper. His first name is Casper. That's why I gave you the card, in case you want to confess."

"I didn't kill him. But let's say I did, why would I confess to you rather than the sheriff?"

"Because I'm nicer."

"Whatever," I said, then opened the door to my car. I was about to get in, again, when I stopped. "Hold on, you say they hired you to prove that *I* killed him? They didn't hire you to find out *who* killed him? It has to be me?"

"Yeah, I have a problem with that too."

"Do you still get paid if you find out someone *else* killed him?"

"Oh, I've already been paid. Twenty-five-hundred-dollar retainer, three hundred a day plus expenses. That'll last seven days. Six, if I eat in nice restaurants."

Okay, that sounded like a racket. I wondered, *where do I sign up?*

To Hamlet, Ham, I said, "So let's say I didn't do it, because I didn't, what do you tell them in a week?"

"More like five days. This is the second day. And I had a big breakfast."

"Right. What are you going to tell them?"

"Everything you do this week. Everything people say about you. The whole shebang really. So... I hear you solved a murder last spring. Got a big reward."

"Yeah, so what?"

"It's just weird that someone who solves a murder turns around and commits one. Doesn't track. You know?"

"You don't think I did it. You're just taking their money."

"Somebody has to, why shouldn't it be me?"

I finally got into my car. He came up to the window and bent over to look at me, "How about you make this easy on me. Where you going?"

I hardly knew until it came out of my mouth, "I'm going to the library to find out more about the Blinski family."

"Okay. I'll be out front."

Driving back to Masons Bay, I tried to remember what Opal said about the Blinskis. Divorced. First wife in Florida. His nurse—Helena? Became his second wife. Lots of kids. Check the phonebook.

The Mason Bay Library was on Main Street at the south end of village in a two-story brick building that had once been a lumbermill—the second time they cut all the trees in the state down. They'd cleaned up the brick and made it look all spiffy.

Inside, the circulation desk was at the front with activity

areas along the sides, including a couple rows of PCs available to the public. The second floor was largely open, basically a deep balcony running around most of the building. It had enough room for a set of bookshelves and a walkway.

At the front desk was a chunky guy named Chad who I'd nicknamed Hanging Chad. When I walked in, I had a notepad that Bev made me carry around even though I told her I didn't need it. Well, now I did.

Hanging Chad saw me and said, "Hey. Glad you came in."

Okay, so he kind of liked me, but... ew, no. Still, I gave him the kind of smoldering look that should send a shiver down his spine and... lo and behold. Then I thought, *Oh crap*. I was cock-teasing a librarian for information. I was as bad as that horrible woman I met in line the other night. I tried to make my face very bland—a challenge, I know.

"I'm looking for information on the Blinski family."

"Oh, yeah, that's so sad. Dr. Blinski murdered. Are you investigating? Is there a reward?"

"Not yet."

"Oh, you're just investigating to be nice. That's so cool."

He tried to smolder me back and I thought, *Oh God, what have I done?* He noticed his look wasn't working and, confused, he moved on. "Anyway, you're in luck. If you'll remember, we haven't catalogued the *Eagle* entirely. But... we have finished the B's. So, our fiche room is in the back corner. I'll go through the catalog and pull the sheets for you."

"Great. Thanks."

I started to walk toward the back, when he said, "Oh, today's *Eagle* is right over there." He pointed toward a seating area with periodicals. "Dr. Blinski is on the front page. The sheriff says they have a suspect but aren't able to charge him yet. But you've probably already read that."

"Yes, absolutely," I lied, then grabbed the current *Eagle*. "I'll just take another look in case I missed something.

In the fiche room, I sat down in front of a huge, odd-looking machine, and read the article. It stated that on Friday, September 5th, Dr. Casper Blinski was discovered dead in his office by a patient. Okay, that wasn't too bad. They didn't use my name or call me a suspect. Things are improving. Maybe. It went on.

The doctor's nurse, Nancy Fisher (44), has stated that the doctor was in the supply closet minutes before the attack, which she heard. It is believed the assailant came and left via the window.

No one had mentioned the thing about the supply closet to me. That was new. Did that give the doctor's killer time to crawl in through the window and wait for him? Is that what happened?

There was also a lot of stuff about how important Dr. Blinski was to the community, how long he'd been a doctor, what a loving father he was... nothing about him being a little loose with the Oxy. The article finished by saying funeral plans had not yet been decided.

Next to the article was an anonymous opinion piece titled "Murder Rate in Wyandot County Skyrockets." The essay attempted to blame the recent murders on the negative influence of big cities. That seemed weird since we were about a four-and-a-half-hour drive from the nearest big bad city. And... two of the three murders were decidedly local. And the third was still a question. It was very unlikely that roving bands of citified folk were driving around the county killing people.

But then I wondered, was that a dig at me? Was this anonymous writer suggesting that *I* was the problem? I came from the big city; were they suggesting I'd somehow egged people on to kill? Well, that was a theory that belonged right up there with Area 51. Speaking of Area 51, I loved *Roswell* and was destroyed when they took it off the air. Anyway...

Hanging Chad came in with a small box holding several bright blue plastic sheets. Each sheet had dozens of tiny white boxes on them.

"There's not a lot," he said. "Only three articles, really. There are a bunch of mentions. And that's about it."

He gave me a list of seven dates, and said, "Why don't I set up the first one for you?"

Leaning over me, getting far too close, he slipped the first plastic sheet in between two glass plates. Then, using dials, he moved the fiche around until the right edition of the *Eagle* came up on the giant screen in front of me. Then he moved through until he found the article, which was a wedding announcement.

On May 25, 1957, Dr. Casper Blinski (28) married Veronica (Ronnie) Flaska (24) at Cheswick Community Church Masons Bay. A reception followed in her parents' home. The best man and matron of honor were Mr. and Mrs. Herbert Lee (Carol).

There was a photo of the couple. Surprisingly, Dr. Blinski was kind of hot as a young guy.

By this point, Hanging Chad had stood up and was reading along. When I looked back at him, ready to move on, he said, "The next five mentions are spaced roughly two years apart, until 1968. I'm pretty sure those would be birth announcements. They have similar page numbers. Then there's nothing until 1980. That might be more interesting since it's in the features section of the paper."

"Okay," I said. I can't say I minded having my own personal librarian.

Hanging Chad swapped out the fiche and worked his magic on the machine. Moments later we were looking at an article that had "Local Doc Celebrates 25 Years." There was a large photo of Dr. Blinski in his mid 50s sitting at the rolltop desk in his exam room. He was no longer hot, that was for sure. He'd gained weight, weight that he would lose at some point before I met him.

Skimming the article, it talked about how he was beloved by his patients, his large family of five children ranging from

12 to 21, his parents Clark and Justine Blinski. *Surely his parents are gone by now*, I thought. They'd be nearly a hundred.

When I finished reading the article, Hanging Chad put in the second to last fiche. It was from October 13, 1989. The headline read "Local Doctor Criticizes HIV Clinic." Basically, Dr. Blinski was attacking the Turley HIV Clinic, which was attached to Mid-land Hospital (then Morley Medical Center) in Bellflower. In the article he was quoted as saying, "As a Christian man, I say you reap what you sow. As a doctor, I say you can't test these people anonymously. You have to expose them and force them to quarantine. They are a risk to the general population and must be segregated."

Great. My dead doctor was a documented homophobe. Yippee.

"Nice guy," Hanging Chad said, sarcastically. "I'm a little less sorry he's dead."

"Yeah."

"Okay, last one," he said, then changed out the fiche.

Dr. Blinski's final appearance in the *Eagle*, prior to his murder was his April 15, 1994 marriage to Helena Johnson (42.) She was a full twenty-three years younger than he was and what they used to call a real fox. There was a mention of her thirteen-year-old son, Wayne Johnson, being at the wedding, but no mention of any of Dr. Blinski's five children. That was suspicious.

"Great, thanks," I said to Hanging Chad then asked, "You have phonebooks, don't you?"

"On the shelves next to the circulation desk."

I walked out of the fiche room and up to the circulation desk. I found the phonebooks next to the desk. There was a phonebook for Detroit Metro Area, which was thick, a smaller one for Grand Rapids, and then a very, very thin phonebook for Wyandot County.

Looking up B-L-I-N-S-K-I in the skinny one, I found six

names. One of them was Casper himself listed at 1728 Mead-owlark Lane. I was clueless about local geography, but I thought Meadowlark Lane was just a few blocks away. I wrote down the five other names and addresses, though right now they didn't make much sense to me.

I was about to slip out without thanking Hanging Chad for his help—I was very late getting back to work, Bev was going to be pissed—but then, there he was.

"It's really a pleasure helping you. I mean, it's always so interesting."

That was my cue to say thank you, which wouldn't have been hard, but instead I asked, "Can you tell me which way Meadowlark Lane is?"

CHAPTER SEVEN

Meadowlark Lane was several blocks from Main Street on the east side of the street. You had to climb a steep hill to get there. It was quickly obvious that the houses on Meadowlark Lane all had views of Lake Michigan. I walked down the street until I found 1728. The property was gated with a brick wall surrounding the plot. The wall was over six feet tall and covered with English ivy. It was at least two lots combined into one or possibly three.

The house was set back behind a near jungle of trees and bushes, and a koi pond. There was a strong Asian influence on the landscaping, but just an influence. The architecture of the house also suggested Asian roots, but mainly in its sparseness. The house was built of wood, with shingled walls and beams which ran inside and outside the house. It was painted a deep chocolate brown with blood red trim. There were two stories and many windows.

It looked like a very expensive home. I wondered how a simple country doctor could afford it. Well, I guess I knew the answer to that. I saw him for ten minutes every two weeks and gave him seventy-five dollars each time. How many times a day did he do that? Could he be making thousands and thousands a month on Oxy prescriptions? Thousands and thousands on top of what he made from his regular patients? Was he doubling his income? Tripling it?

I continued to think about all that as I walked down the hill. I was being stupid. The money for the house probably came from somewhere else. I mean, there weren't even enough people in Wyandot County... Except, there kind of were. I'd looked already. There were a few more than fifteen thousand people in the county. Maybe a thousand of them were his patients. Was that a lot? I had no idea. But let's say two hundred of that thousand were just there for a prescription. Then he'd have time to see more patients. So, maybe he had fifteen hundred.

Then I started doing the math—not my forte. Two hundred times seventy-five is fifteen thousand dollars. He was making that as often as every two weeks. Thirty thousand a month, twelve months a year, nearly four hundred thousand on top of whatever he made from his other patients. That was a lot of money. Really, a *lot* of money.

Were there that many people, two hundred, in Wyandot County doing Oxy? If you'd asked me last week, I would have said, no. But two days after Dr. Blinski's death there was a line outside the local drug dealer's trailer. And that line was made up of pretty average looking people.

And that made me wonder about something. I like to have fun with Oxy, which led to my having a little problem. But the people I saw outside Ronnie Sheck's they weren't taking Oxy because they like the nightlife—I mean, seriously, there wasn't any nightlife to like in Wyandot County. Which made me wonder if Dr. Blinski was, like, overprescribing for simple things like backaches and sore feet. Was he making his own addicts?

I was back at Main Street. I was about to turn toward my car—I really had been gone a long time. Bev was going to be furious... Actually, probably not. She was pretty good-natured.

It was hard to imagine her being anything but mildly annoyed. In that case, I turned in the other direction. There was a real estate agency somewhere nearby, I was sure of it.

The agency was called The Hanson Group, and it was in a very small storefront. Unlike most agencies in Los Angeles, they did not hang neat copies of their listings on their windows. In fact, the first thing I noticed was that the office was very elegant, with thick carpet and a couple of mahogany desks and matching guest chairs. It reminded me of the kind of retail shop in Beverly Hills where they kept most of the merchandise in the back and only brought it out after they determined you could afford it.

An overdressed, very flamboyant woman sat behind one of the desks. Underneath the makeup, the dyed hair, the clunky costume jewelry and the expensive designer dress she was probably older than my grandmother.

"Yes..." she said, barely looking up from whatever she was reading.

"I want to ask a few questions about a property."

"And you are...?"

"Henry Milch." I decided not to ask her to call me Mooch, I doubted we'd become friends.

She looked up. "You're Emma Cole's grandson. The one from California."

"The only one, actually."

"I'm Olly Hanson. You work in Hollywood, don't you?"

"Peripherally," I said, hoping to sound like I was being modest rather than hiding the fact that I'd worked at a Starbucks on Hollywood Boulevard.

"Are you looking for a summer home? Or, does Emma want to downsize? I know she'd want me as her agent. I have a number of people who'd be very interested..."

"No, I'm just curious... how much does a house like 1728 Meadowlark Lane go for?"

"Is Helena thinking of selling? Already? She shouldn't

make a decision like that so soon after a death, but if she did...
She really needs to do that with me. Are you interested in
buying it? Or is it Emma...?"

Her eyes lit up at the prospect of a commission for selling
our farm and another for helping us buy the house on Meadowlark Lane.

"I'm really just curious about the house. It's probably not
the right time for us to make a move."

"Of course. Well, if I were to list that house, I'd list it at six
hundred and not take a penny less than five-fifty. It was only
built a few years ago. Casper built it right after he and Helena
got married. She made every decision. The house is a testa-
ment to their love."

"You've been in the house?"

"Oh yes. Helena hosts a book club once a month. I never
read the books, but I always go. It's catered."

"I bet Dr. Blinski's first house was pretty impressive, huh?"

"Oh my goodness, no. The house he had with Veronica,
where they brought up their kids, that house sold for under
two hundred. And I'm pretty sure he had to give it to Veronica
outright. She sold it when she moved to Florida."

"Are all the kids still in the area?" I asked. The way she
was gossiping I thought she might help me out. I was right.

"Well... the oldest, Lena married a Martindale and they
live out near Gaylord. Then there's Victor he's down near
Detroit, I think. Jacob is still here, over in Bellflower—he
married a Smith girl, don't remember which one. Then there's
Susannah, she's never married; she lives just north of Masons
Bay close to the Indian Reservation. Last is Peter; he lives in
Queens Way Mobile Homes. He hasn't done well for himself."

"None of them moved to Florida with their mom?"

"I think Peter was down there for a year or two, then he
moved back."

That was about all I could think of to ask her, so I said
thanks and started to leave.

"Oh wait, take my card," she said offering her business card. "Please think of me when you're ready to sell the family farm."

I felt like she was carefully avoiding what she really meant, which was that I should call her when my grandmother dies—even though she herself seemed much closer to death.

Then again, she might know the sheriff wanted to charge me with Dr. Blinski's murder, which could result in some very hefty legal bills—which could require the sale of the farm. Like my Nana Cole would do that. Ha! It had never occurred to me before, but real estate agents are a little ghoulish.

When I got back to my car, I noticed the Navigator parked behind me. I walked back and tapped on the passenger window. It slid down. I leaned on the car and asked Ham, "The house on Meadowlark Lane, what's it like inside?"

He smiled at me. I don't know why my question made him happy. I was trying to trick him into telling me if he was working for Helena Blinski. Rather than someone else in the Blinski family.

"The house is lovely inside, very... comfortable, as rich people say. And, yes, I'm working for Helena Blinski."

"It seems like he had a lot more money during his second marriage than in his first. Do you know why?" I asked.

"I have the feeling you do. What did you find out at the library?"

"There are hard feelings about his divorce. His kids weren't at his second wedding. But you could go into the library and find that out yourself."

"Helena already told me. Plus, I had my secretary run off everything you just found plus some. Last year the Blinskis went on an all-expenses-paid trip to Santa Barbara courtesy of the makers of OxyContin."

"Why are you sharing information with me?"

"Because one of two things is going on here. Maybe you're

investigating the doctor's death because you're innocent and you want to prove that."

"I'm not really investiga—"

"You are. The other possibility is that you're guilty and you're running around trying to make it seem like you're not."

"Let's go with the first option."

"Either way, sharing information with you doesn't matter, does it?"

And then he rolled up the window.

"WHERE HAVE YOU BEEN? I was starting to worry that you'd been arrested again," Bev said when I finally got back to the conservancy. See, not angry; worried. Angry would have been better.

"I was never arrested. I was questioned."

"Okay, well, that."

"I'm being followed by a private investigator out of Grand Rapids."

"You're kidding?"

"Yeah, that's my idea of a joke. *Not.* He was hired by Helena Blinski. She wants him to prove I killed her husband."

"Wait, specifically you? She doesn't want to know if it's someone else?"

"That's the impression I got."

"But why would she *want* it to be you?"

"I guess because she knows it's someone else."

She looked me straight in the eye and said, "I'm guessing you want the rest of the day off."

"That would probably help."

"Fine."

I gave her the little camera back and she scrolled through the photos. "Yeah, I have concerns about where they're putting that field. I'll look at the plat map. I might have to get a survey done. They're not going to like this."

Honestly, I couldn't care less. Getting your wrist slapped over a misunderstood property line was nothing like being accused of murder. I left, and on my way to my car I stopped at Ham's Navigator again. He rolled down the window.

"Hey, I'm going home now so you can call it a day."

"Are you going out later?"

"I don't know. Probably not."

"Yeah, I'm gonna grab dinner and then I'll be waiting across the street from your house."

I said 'okay,' and almost walked away. I turned back, and said, "Just so you know... People drive really fast on West Shore Drive. If you want to park at the end of the driveway, go ahead. I don't mind."

"Thanks."

"Don't worry about it."

Don't get the wrong idea. It's not that I care about this person I met like five minutes ago. It's just vehicular fatalities directly across from your house can be very messy and... sad.

I was driving down our driveway ten minutes later. Behind my nana's Escalade sat a purple PT Cruiser. Purple. I pulled to one side so whoever it was could get out. The car didn't belong to any of Nana Cole's friends. I had the fleeting thought she might have called for a new physical therapist, which would be great, but was disappointed when I walked into the kitchen.

Nancy Fisher sat there having tea with my grandmother. She looked odd out of her nurses' uniform, as if the pink blouse with a curlicued collar was some kind of betrayal.

When she saw me, she said, "I thought you said he'd be at work. You promised me—"

I answered for my grandmother. "I got off early. Have the two of you been having a nice chat?"

There were cups of tea in front of them and a plate of

store-bought shortbread cookies—I'd gotten them at Benson's. The teacups were only half empty and it didn't look like many cookies had been eaten. She hadn't been there long.

"We were just talking about Nancy's daughter's wedding," Nana Cole said. "It was in July. Very small."

She was reluctant for a moment, then Nancy said, "We'd planned a bigger wedding but my niece, Jemma's cousin, died of a bee sting a few weeks before."

"Wow that's awful," I said, trying to get Nancy to like me, or at least not think I was a murderer.

"Ally was going to be a bridesmaid. When it happened. We decided to scale everything back and there were just fifty people. It was a bit somber." There was an awkward pause. Then Nancy reached for a more cheerful topic—well, only marginally so. "Emma has been trying to convince me you couldn't have killed Dr. Blinski."

"Thanks, Nana." Her loyalty knew no bounds.

"The whole thing has been a terrible shock for poor Nancy. It's easy to see how she might have gotten confused."

"I didn't say that. I wasn't confused. I'm not confused. I heard what I heard."

I said, "You told the *Eagle* that Dr. Blinski went back to the supply closet shortly before the murder, before I got there. Detective Lehmann didn't mention that."

"I told that to the sheriff. Maybe he didn't tell Detective Lehmann, I don't know."

"There was blood outside, underneath the window. I couldn't have put it there because I never got out the window, did I? It looks like someone climbed out after they killed the doctor. You didn't see them come in, so they must have climbed in through the window while Dr. Blinski was in the supply closet. They'd have been waiting there when he came back."

"No, that's not what happened," she said clearly doubting it even as she said it. "I didn't hear anything until you went back and opened the door. Then I heard the doctor cry out. He said, 'Stop no.' I'm sure of it."

"Um, yeah, I think it was actually me. I know when I fell on him, I said something. It might have been, 'Oh fuck' or 'Fuck no,' I'm not sure."

"Henry," my Nana Cole said prudishly. But seriously, if there's ever a time to say 'Fuck no' it's when you fall on a corpse.

Nancy Fisher looked unsure. "It couldn't have happened that way."

"Why not?"

She didn't say anything. Then I asked, "Do you know what Dr. Blinski went to get out of the supply closet?"

"He was probably getting a coupon for you. It's from the drug company. It means you don't actually have to pay for your drugs. They wanted him to give as many away as he can."

My heart warmed a little toward Dr. Blinski, I mean, he was still a homophobe, but he'd been on the verge of giving me free drugs. I mean, could he really be that bad?

Then I realized my grandmother was staring at me and my cheeks began to burn. The reason for my visit had just been exposed. Well, it wasn't like she didn't know I took pills. She basically told me she knew a couple months ago. But we hadn't talked about it since. There were a lot of things we didn't talk about.

"What were the coupons doing in the supply closet?" Nana Cole asked. "Why weren't they in his desk?"

"He was afraid patients would try to steal them if he kept them in his desk. He felt strongly that all his patients should get the coupons, not just a few."

"It sounds like you were aware the Doctor was prescribing a lot of Oxy?" I asked.

"Yes, the drug rep was always sending us things. Hats. Water bottles. Dr. Blinski was one of the top prescribers in Northern Lower Michigan."

"Was he proud of that?" Nana Cole said.

"I think he was."

"But... people up here don't hurt themselves more than they do in other parts of the state, do they?" she wondered.

"Not to my knowledge, no."

"He was addicting people to drugs, wasn't he?" I said.

"The drug company told him that only a small number of people got addicted. He believed that. He thought he was helping people in pain. His patients were so grateful."

"You're a nurse. Didn't you see that it was wrong?" Nana Cole asked.

"I should have done something, I know. He was just a kindly old GP. He wasn't trained to deal with pain management, and he didn't really distinguish between the patients who were faking pain to get drugs and the ones who really needed his help."

"Well, at least no one got badly hurt," my grandmother said. "No one died."

"No. No one died," Nancy said, relief flooding her face.

CHAPTER EIGHT

Mr. Chips was over in Bellflower sandwiched between an antique store and a place that sold take-out pasties. A pasty was a chewy, doughy, hand sandwich that people up here were crazy about. I just thought they were crazy.

From the street, the bar was simply a window with a Miller sign and a door. If you squinted, you could see a rainbow flag sticker on the window. Inside, it's your basic dive bar: vinyl booths, dartboard, a TV hanging from the ceiling (playing football of all things) and a juke box. It was not, by any stretch of the imagination, my idea of a gay bar. It was more like a loser bar and in Wyandot County that included anyone gay, lesbian, bi or whatever.

I ordered a cosmos, which I swear was nothing but vodka and a splash of cranberry. I looked around the nearly empty bar. There were three or four single men at the bar or wandering around. None of them were attractive, but I was probably going to have to talk to them anyway. In the meantime, there was Opal and her checkered hair sitting in a booth with a tall, sharp-edged guy around my age, Carl Burke.

I took a couple of sips from my drink so I didn't spill it, then I walked across the room. I drew a lot of attention since I was wearing my fashionably ripped jeans, a spiked leather dog collar and a black T-shirt from Hot Topic with a glitter skull on the front, it was extra small and didn't go all the way down to my jeans.

"Hi, Opal."

"Hey. Carl, you remember Henry."

"Hi, Henry."

"You can call me Mooch, if you want to." Then I said to Opal, "Are you going to invite me to sit down?"

"Do we have to?"

Carl had scooched over, though, so I sat. She studied me for a long, uncomfortable moment, and then asked, "Why are you so desperate to have people call you Mooch?"

"It's what people called me in high school."

"And you had a good time in high school?"

"Not exactly."

"So why do you want to be reminded of that?"

She was putting me on the spot. I squirmed. "I don't know. I mean, it doesn't—it's just—if people are going to make fun of you it's better to get there first. That's all."

"Mooch is the coach of the Lions," Carl said, flatly.

"Is that football?"

"Yeah, we're definitely not going to call you Mooch," Opal said.

"Whatever." I was desperate to change the subject, so I asked Carl, "How's your mother?"

His mother was Ivy Greene, whose husband, my grandmother's minister, was murdered a few months before.

"She's okay. She told me you killed Dr. Blinski."

"I didn't. But it's nice of her to think of me." I really was getting tired of being accused of murder.

"Do you think they're going to arrest you soon?" Opal asked. God, this was a cheerful conversation.

"I doubt it. Nancy Fisher claimed she heard me murder him but now she's changed her mind."

Or at least she's almost changed her mind.

"The killer climbed through the window while Dr. Blinski was in the supply closet. When he came back," I made the international symbol of a throat being cut, "then went back out the window. I walked in a few minutes later and fell on his corpse."

"Gross," Carl said.

"Is it weird that she didn't hear the murder? I mean, she heard you," Opal asked.

"I don't know. It probably happened really fast."

That was a good question, though. It got me thinking about that scalpel again. It seemed like something the killer just grabbed, as though they hadn't come there planning to kill the doctor. But, picking up the scalpel in the heat of the moment suggested an argument, which Nancy didn't hear. What she heard was nothing, which implied a carefully planned and executed murder. So they didn't just grab the scalpel. They climbed through the window, took the scalpel out of the desk, and waited.

We'd been quiet for too long. I felt like I should be asking Carl more questions, just to be polite, but all I knew about him was that he was in love with a meth-head barber. I blurted out, "Why are you still here?"

"Me?"

Opal said, "Henry, don't be an asshole."

"I meant, why are you still in Wyandot County? Why not move to a bigger place. Experience the world. Meet more boys. Meet more girls. Whatever."

"I like it here. My mom needs me. I have friends. I have..."

Denny the barber-boy. Yeah, I guess that was a stupid question to ask him.

"When are *you* leaving?" Opal asked.

"Soon. I have my car. My old roommate wants to get an apartment with me again. I just need to bank a little cash. And, you know, not be a murder suspect."

"That car is not going to make it to California."

"What is it?" Carl asked.

"It's a convertible. And it's blue."

"It's a little Japanese lawnmower," Opal said.

"It will get me to California. I'm going to drive slowly, and it will take a few extra days. So what?"

I was planning to drive slowly since I had no real choice. The speedometer only went up to 85. And I suspected that was a lie.

We talked about other things for a while. *Jeepers Creepers 2*, which Opal thought was the most frightening film she'd ever seen—which made Carl giggle; George Bush, who we all agreed was the worst president past, present or future; and a friend of theirs from high school who went into the Navy after 9/11 but changed his mind, and threw away his uniforms and faked a nervous breakdown to get out.

Mostly I focused on hoping one of them would buy me a drink. Neither seemed inclined to do that, so I went up to the bar and got myself another.

Ham had come in at some point and was sitting at the far end of the bar. He winked at me, and I snarled back. I wasn't sure how I felt about being followed. I mean, it did make me feel kind of important, but important wasn't always a good thing.

When I got back to the table, I asked Opal, "Why do you work if you're a trust fund baby?"

"I said I have a little money; I didn't say I was wealthy."

"That's the kind of answer rich people give."

"I like to feel useful, okay?"

"By selling people flouncy dresses and getting them drunk on apple cider?"

"I also volunteer at the Turley Clinic. Something you should think about."

"I have no desire to be useful."

"Yeah, we know."

I took a big gulp of my drink. On the one hand, the hair on my neck had started to stand up in an uncomfortable way and I felt just a little nauseated. It was probably time to split another 10. On the other hand, I was also starting to feel a little drunk and that felt... good. Maybe I could just do that instead and hold off until the morning before I took another half. That would make up for moving in the wrong direction on Sunday, wouldn't it?

"That guy at the bar keeps looking at you," Opal said. "Don't ask me why but I think he's into you."

I didn't even have to turn around. I knew she was talking about Ham.

"Yeah, I don't think he's into me. He's a private detective from Grand Rapids. Helena Blinski hired him to prove I killed her husband."

"That's not how that's supposed to work."

"Ya think? Helena Blinski can't *pick* who killed her husband."

"I mean, if you're being followed by a private eye, you shouldn't know about it," Opal said.

I shrugged. "He introduced himself this morning. I'm sure it's a strategy. Like, if he makes friends with me, I'll just confess."

Actually, he'd basically told me that.

"Do you think Helena Blinski is behind her husband's murder?"

"Kind of, yeah."

"She couldn't have done it herself," Opal said. "She comes into Pastiche. She's in her early fifties and her waist is expanding. I don't think she could climb through a window."

"Someone could have done it for her," I said.

"Or she's protecting someone she *thinks* did it," Carl said.

"That's what *I* think."

I must have been drunk, since the next time I needed a drink I offered to get one for Opal and Carl. They glanced at each other and then Opal said, "Thanks but no. I have work in the morning and Carl's my ride."

"Fine, be that way," I said, drifting away.

I ordered myself another drink and, after it was poured started talking to the guy sitting next to the service station. It was what I'd come for. I was looking for anyone who might have a bit of Oxy on hand that they didn't want. Vicodin would be okay, too. Or anything, except, like, heroin. I feel so much better abusing FDA approved drugs.

Of course, you had to talk to someone for at least a few minutes before you popped a question like that. In the course of the evening, I was offered two blow jobs and the 'ride of a lifetime,' but no Oxy.

I managed to have three more drinks, so I was, as they say, feeling no pain. Rudely, the bartender called last call. I hate that. Always have. I understand opening bars, but I don't understand closing them. Why do they have to close? They should stay open as long as they have people in them.

Unfortunately, it really was time to leave. I walked out onto the sidewalk and there was Ham, Hamlet, Ham. Clearly, he was waiting for me.

"I'm going to give you a ride home," he said.

"What? Don't be stupid."

"You've had six drinks. Very strong drinks."

"Blawch," I said, as though it was a word with meaning. "You've had a lot a drinks, too."

"I had one vodka and tonic and six plain tonics."

"That's not fair."

"I really can't be out driving drunk while I'm working. Let me take you home."

"No. I'm fine. I can drive. You don't need to worry about me."

He took a plastic bag out of his pocket and held it up. It held about twenty medium-sized white pills. Oxy.

"Is this what you've been looking for?"

"I'm not looking for—but yeah, I'll take those."

"Let me drive you home and I'll give them to you in the morning."

"Why can't I have them now? You should give them to me now. That's what a nice person would do."

"Yeah, you could easily overdose and that would be bad for me. You can't die until end of day Friday. I don't want to give any of my retainer back."

"How did you know I wanted those?"

"First of all, Dr. Blinski, duh. And secondly, you asked pretty much every guy in there if they'd recently had dental work, surgery or broken a limb. I'm not gay, so maybe I'm wrong, but those are really shitty pickup lines."

"Shut up."

CHAPTER NINE

So, yeah, he drove me home. I only slept a few hours before I was downstairs in the bathroom puking. Apparently, alcohol was not such a great substitute for Oxy. Who knew? During a pause in the puking, I checked my stash. Ham didn't want to give me any pills because he thought I'd OD. Well, joke's on him, I still had more than enough Oxy to OD on. If I wanted to.

Of course, that was not my plan. I broke a 10 in half, just like I'd planned. I waited until I'd puked a few more times. Then I swallowed the half with a tiny bit of water. Just a few minutes later, the nausea began to build again. I panted, I put a cold washrag on my head, then I lay down on the cool linoleum floor. I did everything I could think of not to puke out the thing that I knew would make me stop puking. The nausea stopped for a few minutes. Then the whole thing started again. It was like that for about an hour. Maybe longer. Then I fell asleep on the bathroom floor.

"Henry, Henry wake up. I have to use the toilet."

I struggled to open my eyes. Through slits, I saw that Nana Cold had pushed the door open about eight inches. It wouldn't go any further because my butt was in the way.

"Give me one second," I said. I pushed the door closed and stood up. I was still a little wobbly. Okay, a lot wobbly.

I looked into the toilet, yuck, and flushed it. I snatched up my stash and put it in my jammies' pocket. Rinsed out the sink —I don't know what happened there—and finally opened the door.

She waddled in, nearly falling into me.

"Sorry," I said.

"Where is your car?" she asked, as she pushed me out of the bathroom, slamming the door as she did.

"Is it in a ditch somewhere?" she yelled through the door.

"No. A friend drove me home," I yelled back.

"There's a car at the end of the driveway. Is that your friend?"

That was too much to explain through the bathroom door, so I yelled, "I'm going into the kitchen."

I walked down the hall to the kitchen and turned the burner on under the kettle. There was no way I was having coffee after the night I'd had. Tea. I would be having tea. Gentler.

A few minutes later, my grandmother came down the hallway, slamming her four-pronged cane into the floor with each step and threatening to fall over. First one way, then the other.

"Is that your friend at the end of the driveway?"

"Okay, so he's not exactly my friend. He's a private detective from Grand Rapids. His name is Hamlet Gilbody."

"That's a ridiculous name. You made it up."

"Why would I do that? Helena Blinski hired him."

"And he brought you home drunk from a bar?" she said skeptically. She wasn't buying this.

"Yes."

"Helena Blinski hired him to bring you home from the bar."

"No, she hired him to prove I killed her husband."

This was a little easier to believe. She absorbed it for a

moment, then propelled herself toward the wall phone, picked up the receiver and began to dial. I went over and broke the connection.

"What are you doing?"

"I'm calling Helena and giving her a piece of my mind."

"You can't do that. I don't want her to know I know she hired a private detective."

"Why not?"

"Because I'm pretty sure he doesn't think I'm the murderer. Honestly, he's just taking her money."

"Oh. Well. I guess she deserves that," she said, hanging up the phone. Then she careened to the table and plopped down.

The kettle was whistling so I made myself a cup of tea with four teaspoons of sugar.

"Do you want toast with that?"

"No. I'm fine," I said. Holding down a cup of tea could prove to be challenging all on its own. Bread wasn't going to help. Not at the moment.

"What are you going to do?" Nana Cole asked.

"I don't know. Wait for it all to blow over?"

She raised an eyebrow at me. That's when I realized she might be as valuable a resource as the library.

"What's the gossip on Dr. Blinski and Helena?"

"That he's a sweet old man and she's a gold-digging slut," she said, her hand flying up to cover her mouth when she said slut. "I mean, that's what people say."

"So you think he was having an affair with his second wife while he was still married to his first?"

"Everyone thinks that."

"But that's not what a sweet old man would do?"

"I'm sure she bewitched him."

"When a married man has an affair, it's the fault of the woman he has the affair with?"

"Of course. If she'd just said no there wouldn't be an affair."

Okay, that was weird. I mean, to me it was clearly the fault of the person who'd made the vows. Or at least mostly the person who'd made the vows, much more than the person who helped break them. But fine. I moved on.

"What about her son? What's his story?"

"Wayne?" She shook her head. "That poor boy. He married a migrant worker's daughter when he was seventeen. She was pregnant, of course. He was a father at eighteen. And then, at nineteen he went to prison. Pot. He was caught with several pounds."

The irony of my doctor/dealer's stepson going to prison for dealing was not lost on me.

Nana Cole continued, "Helena spent a fortune on lawyers. But it didn't help."

"Does Wayne's wife still live in the area?"

"I don't think so. Helena didn't like that she had a little brown grandchild. She wasn't much help."

"I don't think you should call a child brown like that."

"Why? President Bush, the first one I mean, said it about his own grandchildren."

"Really?"

"You were just a baby."

I frowned at her. "Yeah, you know, a few things have changed since the eighties."

She shrugged like I was being ridiculous.

Then I had to ask a question, something awkward that had been bothering me. "It seems like everyone knew Dr. Blinski was prescribing too many pills. Did you know?"

"Of course not. I'd never have taken you there if I knew what he was up to."

"Really? Don't take this the wrong way, but you're really good at gossip."

I could see her struggle for a moment, trying to decide if she should say 'thank you.' Instead, she said, "I'm not sure how much my friends knew about that. They all knew I really liked

Dr. Blinski, trusted him. If they did know I'm not sure they'd have told me."

That made sense.

I sipped my tea and thought about everything she'd said. Money, the house, the lawyers, Dr. Blinski always needed lots of income to give to Helena. They couldn't have saved much. And now he was getting older. Or had been before...

Was Helena afraid he'd die and the money would run out? Was there an insurance policy? Would she be able to sell his practice? How much was a medical practice worth?

Also, who could have done it for her? Her son was in prison, and I don't think murdering your stepfather qualified for work release. I needed to connect Helena to someone able to climb through the window, slit the doctor's throat, and climb back out again.

I drank the rest of my tea, then said, "I'm going to take a shower and go get my car."

"Should I call Bev and tell her you're not coming in?"

"I think she'd be very surprised to see me today."

I SQUINTED at the blindingly gorgeous morning as I walked down my grandmother's long driveway and climbed into the Navigator. It was quite plush. Like the waiting room in a decent lawyer's office. Ham was dressed for a morning of golf, which matched perfectly with the SUV. I suppose it was his way of remaining nondescript.

"How do you feel?" he asked.

"Like I've recently been thrown out of a moving vehicle. You did come to a complete stop when you dropped me off last night?"

"You don't remember?"

"I remember you have some Oxy and you said you'd give it to me this morning."

He took a plastic bag of Oxy out of his pocket. It was about half of what he showed me the night before. "Where's the rest of it?"

"You'll get it another time."

"I promise I won't take it all at once. I'm titrating down. I'm taking 20 mils a day. Next week I'm going down to 10. Or 15."

Well, hopefully. I was already thinking the following week might be better.

"I'll give you the rest later. What are you going to do now?"

"Get my car. Later when?"

He ignored me and asked, "After you get your car, then what?"

"I should probably talk to the Blinski kids. Ask some questions about the family. In particular, their stepmother."

"Good choice."

"My grandmother was telling me about Helena Blinski and her son, Wayne Johnson. She's been spending a lot of money. For years. Do you know if Dr. Blinski had life insurance?"

"Helena didn't mention it, but I can't imagine why there wouldn't be insurance."

"You can't find out?"

"There's no database. I've heard talk about putting one together, but I can't just get onto the computer and find out. Not yet." He started the SUV and pulled out onto West Shore Drive. "I can make some assumptions though."

"Like?"

"It's only been five days. She might not have a death certificate, yet which means she couldn't file a claim even if she wanted to. But since the certificate is going to say death by homicide, she probably won't want to file a claim until the killer is caught because they'll start an investigation and that will go on forever."

"Do you think that's why she wants you to prove I'm the killer?"

"Could be. I don't know. Either she's responsible and she wants you to take the rap. Or she knows who's responsible and she wants you to take the rap instead of them. Or she's just greedy and wants you to be arraigned so she can file for her money. Or some combination of all three."

"Can you assume anything else?"

"I assume the policy is big. He was making a lot of money."

"More than a quarter of a million a year."

"Really, that much?"

I nodded but didn't explain. I mean, my math could be wrong and that would be embarrassing. The drive to Bellflower was nearly a half an hour. I wondered what I'd said to him the night before when he drove me home. I wondered what I should say to him now.

"What made you decide to be a private investigator?" Seemed like a good question.

"Family business. My dad is a PI in Chicago."

"Really? Why aren't you working for him?"

"I did for a while, but we don't mix. Oil and water."

"Yeah, that's like me and my mother."

"I know. I've heard all about it."

"You have?"

"I'm staying at a bed and breakfast in Masons Bay. Dolores Abbott runs it. She says you and her daughter Cheryl Ann are an item."

"Which should tell you how reliable her information is."

"She says your mother has always got a different boyfriend."

"A couple of them were actual husbands."

"She's kind of a flake. Not really what you'd call a good mom."

"How would Dolores know *that*? I grew up in Los Angeles. Mostly."

I mean, I knew that my mother wasn't great. I didn't know *everyone* knew. Whatever feeling I had for my mother was coming to the surface. Like, *I* could say she was a crappy mom, but I didn't like other people saying it. Strangely, I felt like I had to defend her.

"My mom's big problem is that she has super bad taste in men. I mean, some of them really seemed okay at first, but then eventually things would go sour. Bad things would happen and then we'd move. Sometimes it was more like hiding, but mostly we just moved."

"And you don't think your mom was responsible for a lot of that?"

"I just said she has bad taste in men."

The silence that followed somehow drove his point home. Yeah, okay, maybe it was all more her fault than I remembered, but how was I to know. I only ever heard her side of it.

"What about your father?"

"I don't know who he is."

"Your mother never told you?"

"She doesn't know either. He was like a two-night stand."

"She spent two whole days with someone and she never got his name?"

"I get the impression they were busy."

"Have you asked a lot of questions?"

"Let's back up. My mother has really, really bad taste in men. Why would I want to know who my father is? It feels like asking for another bad stepfather. One I'd never get rid of."

"Sorry, it's my nature to ask questions."

"You think we might be long-lost brothers?" I teased.

"I don't think so. I know who my parents are."

I didn't think we were long-lost anything. But that made me think I could have long-lost siblings or other family members floating around somewhere in California. Did I want to find them? Absolutely not. Just thinking about them filled me with dread.

CHAPTER TEN

I decided to see Peter Blinski first since he lived in Queens Way Mobile Home Park and I knew exactly how to get there. Also, since he lived in a trailer park I thought he might be home on a Tuesday morning. Maybe that's a little prejudiced, I wasn't sure, and I didn't really want to know. I just hoped he was at home.

Anyway, when I got out there at around ten-thirty in the morning, I couldn't believe my eyes. There were cars up and down the street and there was still a line outside Ronnie Sheck's trailer. Wow, Dr. Blinski's death was really having an effect on the community. I parked behind a little Nissan truck.

Ham was already parked down the street and sitting in his Navigator. He didn't have the patience to follow behind me. I mean, it was understandable, I didn't go very fast. Which might have been why he's been so cordial. He simply couldn't stand the idea of trying to follow a slowpoke like me.

From the number, I figured the trailer was at the far end of the park. It was probably a bit much to call it a park. It was one single street with seven trailers on each side. Given the age of some of them, my guess was the land was sold off from a nearby farm before zoning laws were a thing. And definitely before the land conservancy.

Peter Blinski's mobile home was at least thirty years old. It had an industrial-sized bay window on the front but tiny windows everywhere else. Most of it was white, but there was a daring pink stripe down the sides. A stack of concrete blocks made a front stoop. I climbed it and knocked on the door.

A few moments later, a man in his mid-thirties opened the door behind the metal screen door. He was unkempt, needed a shave (and not in that sexy five o'clock shadow way). He had a bad case of bedhead and wore a yellowing T-shirt with a history of stains going back at least a month.

"Hi," I said brightly, my cheerfulness increased by his ickiness. "I'm Henry Milch, Mooch, I was a patient of your father's and I want to talk about your stepmother."

"I know who you are. People are saying you killed my dad."

"Yeah, except I didn't."

Seriously, this guy looked like he might not have left his trailer since the year 2K, and he still hears the gossip?

"Don't worry. No one in my family is upset if you did."

"Good to know. But I still didn't."

"Whatever."

I thought about asking him to let me in so we could sit down, but behind him I could see the fake maple paneling of his living room and the fake yellow paneling of his kitchen, the stacks of *National Geographic* and *National Enquirer*, a gun cabinet and a molting stuffed dear head. Not to mention the smell that drifted out of the place.

"You know what's going on down at Ronnie Sheck's?" he asked me. I decided, despite the décor, he was probably not a drug addict.

"Some kind of party. Can you tell me about your stepmother?"

He stared at me a long time, trying to decide if he should

talk to me, then he shrugged. "She was okay at first. Like a part of the family for a while. She used to spend the holidays with us. Thanksgiving. Christmas. Her and her son, Wayne. He was a weird kid."

The last seemed kind of ironic since it was obvious Peter himself was a weird kid.

"Do you know how long your dad was having an affair with her before your parents divorced?"

"Long time. We all sided with Mom when we found out. I mean, if he'd been more honest maybe we wouldn't have, but it felt like he cheated on all of us, you know?"

Honestly, I did not. My mother was more often the home-wrecker than the home-wreckee. Still, I nodded sympathetically, as though I did know how he felt.

"I was supposed to go to college. My father promised all of us he'd send us to college. But then he met her, and she took everything."

That seemed off to me. At school, I knew people who only had college funds *because* their parents divorced. It was part of the settlement. And then I tried doing some math in my head. As I've said, a struggle, but I was pretty sure Peter had been beyond college age when his parents divorced.

Was he saying Dr. Blinski was giving his nurse money well before his marriage ended? Maybe I should ask. "It sounds like you're saying your dad was spending a lot of money on Helena even before the divorce. Is that true?"

"My mother really wanted to work it out. They were separated for a long time. We kept telling her to get a lawyer and she didn't. Growing up it seemed like he made a lot of money, but then when they divorced he was suddenly broke. Then he and Helena got married and he had lots of money again. It was really unfair."

"You ever hear anything about your dad over-prescribing medications?"

"Yeah, people said things." His brow creased. "You weren't being honest. Ronnie Sheck's not having a party, is he?"

"No, he's not."

"You ever feel like things are all your fault, even when they're not?"

"No. Things usually *are* my fault even when I pretend they're not."

I walked back out to Turtle Highway, then down to Ham's SUV. I told him I was going to Jacob Blinski's and then we drove over to Bellflower. Once again, he got there long before I did.

Jacob Blinski lived on Second Street, one of the nicest streets in Bellflower. It was right down the street from Sammy Hart's house. His was a white, two-story Victorian with a wide wraparound porch. I climbed the steps and rang the bell. Nothing happened, so I rang it again.

Finally, the Smith girl opened the door. She was pretty, blonde and just into her thirties. She wore exercise clothes, and I had the feeling I might have interrupted her workout.

"Hi. My name is Henry Milch. Mooch," I smiled in a friendly way. "Is Jacob Blinski in?"

"He's at work. I'm Sally, his wife. What's a Mooch?"

"Nickname."

She grimaced, but said, "Come on in," opening the door wider so I could enter. I couldn't help but think this was awfully easy.

The parlor was lovely. The flower-print sofa was over-stuffed and inviting. The little tables surrounding it were probably antiques. The wallpaper was a subtle bamboo pattern in peach and the drapes matched. At one end, there was an arched entrance into the formal dining room.

"Can I get you something? Evian? Pellegrino?"

Water? What did she think, I needed to take a pill? I didn't, by the way. I was still hours away from my next half

Oxy. What I really wanted was something with sugar, but from the looks of her I doubted she had anything as simple as a cola.

"Thanks, I'm fine."

"Have a seat then," she said. I sank into the sofa while she perched on a chair that looked like something out of Versailles. "I don't think you killed him, by the way."

Which explained why she'd invited me in.

Shaking her head, she said, "No. It's really unlikely."

"Well, that's a relief," I said.

"You know, I could really use a Gatorade. Are you sure you don't want anything?"

"Actually, I'll have a Gatorade if you have enough."

"Of course."

Looking around it seemed like she probably had enough of just about everything you could think of. Gatorade was a really good idea. I was still dehydrated. All I'd had was a cup of tea and several glasses of water. I was smoothing out thanks to the half an Oxy I took, but I still had a bit of a headache and it felt like my heart was pumping mud through my veins.

Sally came back and handed me a glass of Gatorade. A glass! I was hoping she'd bring me a whole bottle. I drank half of it down. She sipped hers.

I took a deep breath and asked, "Out of curiosity why don't you think I killed Dr. Blinski?"

"Given the long list of people who had a reason to kill him, I'd say you barely made it on."

"And... who else would be on that list?"

"Oh God, both of his wives, all of his children—except my husband, I know where he was—a few of his patients. I mean, that's like a dozen people right there."

The windows in the parlor were very large and the drapes were open so I didn't even have to get up to say, "Do you see the black SUV a few houses down?"

"Um, yeah. Why?"

"That's a private detective out of Grand Rapids. Helena hired him to prove I'm the one who killed your father-in-law."

"Did she? Do you think she did that because she killed him herself?"

"Whoever did it crawled through a window. A pretty high up window. She's like, in her fifties, right?"

"She is."

"Someone had to have done it for her."

"Oh, you're right. My guess would be her Pilates instructor, Robbie Jensen."

"Tell me why?"

"They're involved. Have been for a long time."

She was right. A Pilates instructor would be able to climb through a window.

"Do you think your father-in-law knew about the affair?"

"Oh God, I have no idea. I never met him."

It didn't seem like an unreasonable question. She knew about the affair, after all. And she wasn't—

"So how do you know about Helena and her Pilates instructor?"

"Robbie used to be *my* Pilates instructor—oh God, not the way that sounds. I mean, I saw them together. Helena's appointment was right before mine and, well, it was completely obvious what was going on. I walked into the studio and then turned around and walked out. And I never went back. It just... it felt like a betrayal to keep going there."

"Your husband hates his stepmother that much?"

"It might seem silly. I know families are supposed to love each other no matter what."

That was probably *not* a great idea, but I decided I wouldn't mention it.

"Oh, I can't tell you what a relief it is to talk about all this. It's sort of a forbidden topic with Jacob and the rest of the family. They all act like their father never existed. Sometimes I just want to scream, your father lives fifteen minutes away, you can't pretend he doesn't exist! Sooner or later, you're going to run into him at Meijer!"

CHAPTER ELEVEN

When I left Sally Blinski, I walked down to Ham's SUV and tapped on the window. When it rolled down, I said, "I think I need lunch."

"There's a sandwich place a couple blocks away on Lakeshore. It's called The Green Goddess. Let's go there."

The window rolled up and left me wondering, how did he know his way around so well? As far as I knew he'd only been there a few days while I'd been there for almost nine months. I was practically a native. Wasn't I?

The Green Goddess was a sandwich shop on the west side of Lakeshore in a narrow storefront. A deli-type counter took up most of the space in the front. In the back were about fifteen booths and tables. The floor was wooden and well-worn, the walls were painted a true avocado green, which should not come as a surprise given the name of the place.

When we walked in, a harried waitress said, "Anywhere you can find..." The place was busy, and she looked to be alone. There was a tiny table in the corner that hadn't been bussed yet, so we grabbed that.

Menus were already on the table, stuck between squeezable mustard and ketchup containers. Next to them, salt and pepper, and a cup full of silverware wrapped in paper napkins. Ham pushed the previous diners' plates to the edge.

Given the name of the place, I feared there would be nothing but veggie burgers and green salads. I was happily surprised to find a cherry Rueben sandwich. Everything in Wyandot County had to have cherries, sometimes that was a mistake and sometimes not. I had high hopes for the sandwich.

"Tell me what you thought of Dr. Blinski," Ham said, while we waited for the waitress.

"Well, his family hated him and—"

"No, I mean what *you* thought of him. I never got to meet him. You did."

"Yeah, but..." Once again, I found myself doing math in my head. Why did that happen so often? I'd seen him maybe ten or twelve times. For ten minutes, tops. "All together I think I saw him for like two hours total. That's not enough time to get to know someone."

"You'd be surprised," he said.

"Yeah, but... most of what we said to each other was 'hi,' 'yes it still hurts,' and 'bye.' I mean, he was nice enough. He never made me beg."

Yes, I would have begged if I had to. Give me a break.

The waitress arrived and we ordered. I got the cherry Rueben I was looking at; Ham ordered a fried perch sandwich. I asked for a cherry cola, a glass of water and an Arnold Palmer.

Ham gave me the side eye and said, "Thirsty?" To the waitress he said, "I'll just have water."

She hurriedly bussed the table and walked away.

"Do you mind if I ask some questions about your visit to Dr. Blinski?"

"Um, sure," I said, wondering if this was the part where he tried to pin the murder on me. I mean, it seemed like he believed me, but he might have been lulling me into a false sense of security.

"Walk me through the other day."

"My appointment was at one o'clock, which is about when I got there. I went in a few minutes later."

"Were there other patients in the lobby?"

"Um, no. It was right after lunch."

"Do you usually go at one?"

"No. It was all they had."

"When you walked back, did you hear or see anyone else? Do you think there were patients in the other exam rooms?"

"There's only the one exam room."

"Really?"

"Yeah, he's like a country doctor."

"Were there usually other patients in the lobby?"

"Usually, yes."

"Do you think he scheduled in fifteen-minute intervals? Were you ever asked to be there at say two-fifteen?"

"Maybe. I don't really remember."

"Did you always get in on time?"

"No. Sometimes I had to wait. But never very long."

Ham nodded. "He was probably scheduling three pill patients every fifteen minutes. Segregating them from his other patients."

"I was the only one there on Friday."

"That's beginning to seem odd."

The waitress brought our drinks, mostly mine. I drank three quarters of the cherry cola before she'd set the other drinks down. Before she walked away, I said, "I'm going to need a refill."

She stared at me like I was some kind of freak, and then walked away.

Ham asked, "How did you end up here? You're from L.A., aren't you?"

"I came to take care of my grandmother. She had a stroke."

"Yeah, try again."

"What do you mean, try again?"

"You're lying. Tell me the truth."

I sighed heavily. Then drank the rest of my cherry cola until the straw made it gurgle. "I took one Oxy too many and sort of OD'd. It was a huge misunderstanding and I had to choose between rehab and coming here."

He shook his head. "It doesn't work that way. You're an adult."

"That's the rumor, yeah. Look, I know it doesn't work that way *now*. But I was messed up at the time and my mother told me I had to choose between rehab and my Nana's farm. No one contradicted her. I was in the hospital for three days and I think I saw a psychiatrist for a total of a half an hour. Yeah, I eventually figured out I could have just gone home. That I didn't *have* to be here. But by then I was here. Stuck."

Explaining that made me want to kill my mother. For like the millionth time.

"Why do you think your mother did that to you?"

"Because she has a really messed up idea of what it means to be a parent."

"You don't think it was tough love?"

"More likely she just didn't want to deal with me."

"It could have been both."

That was a weird thing to say. It kind of pissed me off. It was like he was saying my mother was a good mother and bad mother at the same time. Which was completely impossible.

It seemed like a good idea to change the subject. "I guess Helena Blinski was having an affair with her Pilates instructor, Robbie. We should check him out. He could probably climb through that window."

"She."

"What do you mean she?"

"I mean Robbie is a she. Helena is having an affair with a woman."

"Oh. How do you know?" And before he could answer, I did it for him. "Dolores Abbott."

"Actually, her daughter, Cheryl Ann. I get the impression Dolores doesn't think lesbians exist."

"The sheriff's department should really hire them both."

"So, killer lesbians. Sexy, huh."

"Not if you're the one they kill."

"Ah, but what a way to die."

I rolled my eyes at him. Straight guys.

"So, now what?" he asked.

I shrugged. I kind of had no idea.

"Well... What if it was Robbie the Pilates instructor who climbed through the window and killed him. How do we prove that?"

"You tell me."

"Um, well, fingerprints."

"She probably wore gloves. She climbed through the window, so it was planned. That means she probably wore gloves."

"Her clothes are covered in blood."

"The clothes are gone. Burned in someone's backyard or buried out in the state park somewhere."

"There's probably blood in her car."

"That's possible. If she's smart, she put a garbage bag over her seat. And then paid to have it detailed."

"Okay," I said. "This is a lot. In the middle of the day, she crawled in and out of a window, walked to her car covered in blood, put a garbage bag over the seat, and then drove away. And no one saw that?"

"Should we go there after this? Take another look at things?"

I wasn't sure anyone had taken a first look.

"Yeah, not a bad idea."

OKAY, the cherry Reuben was fabulous. On top of that I managed to drink about a gallon of fluids. After a quick trip to the restroom, we left for Masons Bay. Ham would get there first, of course. It would be very interesting to see what kind of report he wrote. What would today sound like?

Would he write that he spent the night spying on me? Though I think he went home for most of it and just returned early in the morning. Would he then say he followed me to Bellflower? Then out to Queens Way, where he observed me talking to Peter Blinski? Then he followed me back to Bellflower and observed me entering Jacob Blinski's house at his wife's invitation?

And what about lunch? He picked up the check saying he was going to expense it. Which means that Helena Blinski paid for my lunch even though she's desperate to prove I murdered her husband. Ironic. Or weird. Or something.

When I got to Masons Bay, Ham was already parked behind the doctor's office. He was out of his Navigator snooping around. I parked and walked over.

"I need to pee again," I said. "Where do you think there's a bathroom?"

"Cup of Mudd, probably."

That was like four blocks away. I suppose I could drive but...

"Just go behind a bush."

"Are you crazy?"

"It's not a big deal."

"You just want me to pull my dick out."

He rolled his eyes.

"All right, I was thinking of doing this anyway." He walked over to the backdoor of the house Dr. Blinski used for his office. There were actually two doors, one for the doctor's office and the other for the apartment which took up part of the first floor and all of the second. Fortunately, the apartment looked dark and empty. I had no idea if anyone lived there.

Ham pulled a couple of small, black metal strips out of his pocket and in two seconds he'd opened the door to Dr. Blinski's office.

"Wow, that's impressive," I couldn't help saying. "I want to do that. You need to teach me."

"Some other time, go pee."

I walked in. Of course, it was still a crime scene so we shouldn't be there. The bathroom was right there next to the backdoor. Using my sleeve, I opened the door and went in. It seemed to take forever to empty my bladder. Since I was dehydrated, you'd have thought I'd keep more of the fluid in my body.

When I came out of the bathroom, I poked around looking for Ham. Across from Dr. Blinski's office, the door of which was currently closed, was a station with a sink for washing your hands, cabinets up and down filled with doctor-y things. Tongue depressors, gloves, bandages, swabs, cotton balls. Many of these things he also kept in his exam room so I kind of wondered if they were there for decoration.

I found Ham at Nancy Fisher's desk digging through the files with gloved hands.

"What are you doing?"

"It doesn't look like they took the doctor's files. Which was kind of dumb if you ask me."

"Are you going to take them?"

"No. One of these people might be his killer. We don't want to mess with real evidence."

"But isn't that what you're doing?"

"We don't want to mess with evidence in such a way that they know. They won't ever know, right?"

"I'm very good at secrets."

I was total crap at secrets, but he didn't need to know that.

"Robbie Jensen was a patient."

"Really? What's it say?"

He took the file out and started to hand it to me. He noted

my ungloved hands and, with a frown, set the file on the counter. He nodded toward a box of gloves on the station behind me, I grabbed a pair and put them on. Not as bad as a condom, but still, not fun. Sweaty and uncomfortable.

Handing me the file he said, "He wasn't giving her Oxy." Ignoring that, I opened the file. It was pretty thin. He'd treated her for a bad flu in 2002. Before that, he'd done a full physical which had had something to do with an insurance policy. Her first visit had been about genital herpes in 2001. Ew, ick.

"Is my file in there?"

"Haven't seen it."

"You think the only file they took was mine?"

"Possibly."

"Is my grandmother's file in there?"

He pulled out a thick file and held it out to me.

"Do you think she might have climbed through the window and killed the doctor?"

I rolled my eyes. "Is that sarcasm?"

He shrugged. "Just asking. Are you sure you want to invade her privacy."

"She lies to me. I'm sure of it."

He kept staring at me.

"Seriously? We just broke in here and you're pawing through people's medical records. *Now* you have ethics?"

"She's your grandmother. You might find out things you don't want to know."

He did have a point. If my Nana Cole had genital herpes, I really did not want to know. I handed him back the file. He kept reading names and then pulling them out to check inside. I decided to leave him to it and look around.

I went back to the exam room and pushed the door open. The blood was all still there on the floor and walls, no one had cleaned it up. The room smelled like the butcher counter in a Mercado you didn't really want to shop at. There was a line in the blood where the scalpel had lain. Which raised the question again, why didn't the killer take it with them? Yeah, I know it would be bad to put it in your pocket, but they could have thrown it out the window and picked it up.

Okay, yeah, sometimes it takes me a while to see the obvious. Which brings me back to why did they leave it? And how did they know which drawer it was in? Helena Blinski would have known. She was his nurse before Nancy. She could have told Robbie where the scalpel was kept. Clearly the killer knew. Right?

Which reminded me, I wanted to look in the supply closet. I walked to the back of the building. The supply closet was next to the bathroom. It was a wide closet with double doors. I opened them both to expose about six shelves. Six shelves full of drugs.

I saw boxes of Crestor, Metformin, Zoloft, Zyrtec, Cialis, Nexium... I went back. Cialis. That was like Viagra—not a problem I had, mind you, but often a valuable trade. I snuck a couple boxes into my jacket. Prevacid, Allegra, Nexium. Interesting. No OxyContin or Vicodin. And where were the coupons Nancy talked about? I scanned the shelves again.

Crap. I wanted a couple or a stack. I mean—wait—I was titrating down. I didn't need discounts on a drug I wouldn't be taking in a few months. Weeks. Soon. Really soon.

That made me count the hours until I could take another half. Actually, I could take one soon. Two o'clock. About twenty minutes away. That merited another trip to the restroom, and I was about to...

When I heard Ham say, "Shit," very quietly. Then, he was crawling down the hallway on his hands and knees. That's when I heard the front door open. I carefully shut the closet doors, then pressed myself against the wall. A moment later, Ham was next to me. Neither of us could be seen from the front.

We listened carefully. Footsteps, a file drawer being opened. The sound of files being slapped onto the counter.

Quite a lot of them. The drawer closed, another opened. More files.

I felt like I might sneeze. I squeezed my nose. Ham saw that and slapped his hand over my face, covering both my nose and my mouth. He put his other hand behind my head. I couldn't breathe. Just my luck to be suffocated while hiding in a doctor's office.

Ham made a decision. He hissed into my ear, "Run." And then, he let go of me. I immediately sneezed. A giant, roaring noise. He grabbed me and we ran out the back door. When we reached the Navigator, we turned and stared at the doctor's back door. No one came out. That meant they'd run out the front while we ran out the back.

So, who was it? And why were they taking files?

CHAPTER TWELVE

After that, I decided to call it a day. It was time for my half 10 and I was starting to feel a little edgy. Plus, I was scared shitless. I had no idea who that was who'd nearly caught us trespassing on a crime scene. I mean, yeah, they ran out the front door when they heard us, but that didn't mean they didn't have a gun. Just because someone chooses not to shoot you doesn't mean you weren't in danger. Whoever it was, was probably covering something up, which meant they were somehow involved in Dr. Blinski's murder.

"You're serious, you're going to go home and stay there?" Ham asked.

"That's what I just said."

"Can I trust you? You're not just trying to shake me."

"You know, I'm not really investigating this."

"Yeah, it seems like you are."

"Well, I mean, I am trying to stay out of prison." Though they seemed to have stopped dragging me in for questioning. So maybe...

"Promise me you're going home and staying there."

"I promise."

He gave me a dubious look, then said, "I'm going out to

talk to Lena Martindale, Dr. Blinski's daughter. There was a file on her. She'd visited her father twice in the last year."

"Really? I bet she doesn't want her family to know about that."

"Or her husband."

"What makes you say that?"

"She paid cash and got a prescription for Zoloft."

"He made his own daughter pay?"

Ham shrugged. "That's something I'm going to ask about."

After that, I drove home. Parking behind my grandmother's Escalade, it was just easier to go in through the front porch, something I didn't do too often. Something I'd probably stop doing in a couple of months, since it would mean shoveling two paths through the snow.

When I walked in, I heard voices. I told myself it had to be Bev or another of my nana's friends. There was a suitcase on the porch, which was new. Or maybe it wasn't. Couldn't exactly remember.

Then I was walking down the hall, with a sick feeling in my stomach. In the kitchen, sitting at the table with my grandmother was... my mother.

It had been more than eight months since I'd seen her. She looked pretty much the same. She was the kind of woman straight guys really went for: long, wispy, blonde hair (professionally dyed, of course. I've seen the roots.) Her eyes were the same soulful brown as mine. The same as Nana Cole's. Usually, she bordered on waifish, but now her cheeks were fuller and, meanly, I hoped she was starting to gain weight.

"What are you doing here?"

"I'm happy to see you, too, sweetheart," she said with a big smile. "You look taller."

"That's not medically possible." Wow, I paid more attention in my anatomy class than I remembered.

"I didn't say you *were* taller, I said you *looked* taller."

"Whatever."

"Henry, would you put the kettle on? I'd like another cup of tea," Nana Cole said. She looked as though she might be in shock. Was she that surprised to see my mother? I mean, I was, but that didn't mean Nana Cole hadn't been warned—

"I can do it," my mother said getting up and walking the few steps to the stove. I gasped. She was hugely pregnant.

"What the—how... Please tell me that's a very large, benign tumor?" I said, somewhat nonplussed. Well, very nonplussed.

"Obviously I'm pregnant," she said, turning the burner on.

"How can you be pregnant? You're too old."

"I'm in my late thirties."

"You're forty-three."

"My *very* late thirties."

"I think the two of you should sit down so we can talk about this calmly," my grandmother said. "There are things we should at least attempt to talk about rationally—"

"Really, Mother? I'm having a baby. There's nothing to talk about. It's far too late to change my mind."

I sat down at the table; she didn't.

"This is the time a family comes together," Nana Cole said. "The mistakes we've made don't matter. It's time to band together and get through this. Emily, you need us."

"What about your boyfriend with the yacht?" I asked.

"What about him?"

"Did you break up?"

"We love each other deeply."

"Is he here, too?"

"He's a very busy, very important man."

"Who can't take a vacation?"

"Coming here was a spontaneous decision."

"Ah." I'd heard that one before. "You ran away."

"I wouldn't call it that. And stop giving me the third degree. I'm not a criminal. I'm a pregnant woman who came to see her mother and her son. There's nothing wrong with that."

She was right, of course, but she was also my mother. She

had a gift for making truly absurd things sound completely reasonable.

I looked at Nana Cole and asked, "Do you know what's going on?"

"Not a clue. All she would say before you got here was how much she missed us."

"Well, that was clearly a lie."

"It's not a lie, Henry. I miss you both terribly. Every day."

Nana Cole gave her a distrustful look but kept her mouth shut.

The tea kettle began to whistle. My mother brought it over to the table and poured them both another cup. After she put the kettle back on the stove, she sat down. I got up and took a cup out of the cupboard and dropped a tea bag into it. Then I attempted to pour water from the kettle, but she'd poured it all. I refilled the kettle and put it back on the stove. I turned the burner on. As I did that, I asked my mother, "How long are you staying?"

"How long are *you* staying," she asked right back.

"Not long. My old roommate in Los Angeles wants to get an apartment with me again. Now that I have a car I'll be leaving soon."

"You can't—" my grandmother said.

"And how soon is soon?" my mother asked.

"He can't leave town until the sheriff says so. He's a suspect in Dr. Blinski's murder."

"Person of interest," I corrected her.

"Dr. Blinski's dead?" My mother said. "Wow, I can't believe that. He gave me my first prescription for birth control."

"Did you forget how they worked?"

My Nana Cole decided to change the subject, "Henry can stay as long as he wants to. This is his home as much as it is yours."

"I wasn't trying to rush him out. He's my son. I think I'm entitled to know his plans."

"Nice of you to take an interest."

"When is the baby due?" my grandmother asked.

"A few weeks maybe. Soon. I was smaller than this when I had Henry. God, I feel like it's shredding my internal organs."

"Wait. You don't know when your baby is due? Haven't you been to a doctor?" I asked.

"That's such a racket. They want to see you every five minutes and take all these tests. They just want your money."

"So, you could be having twins, or an alien or the devil's child?" Okay, so I've seen a few horror movies.

She gave me a look of disgust, and said, "Women have been having babies since the beginning of time. The whole thing goes a lot better if men don't get involved."

"All right, get a female doctor."

"Why? So you can kill her, too?"

"I didn't kill anyone."

"He didn't, Emily. He couldn't."

"Thank you, Nana."

I think that was a compliment, though she might have also been noting that I was probably too cowardly or incompetent to kill someone, which would not be a compliment. Though not far from the truth.

And then, it all fell into place. My mother had promised her boyfriend would pay Vinnie's rent and the check kept bouncing, they lived full time on a boat, but she never mentioned a house or even an apartment, and now she was here to have her baby... so her mother could pay for it.

"He's broke, isn't he? David is broke."

"Absolutely not. It's just the weather. The weather hasn't been going his way."

"What is she talking about?" Nana asked me.

"Her boyfriend gambles on the weather."

"It's not gambling. They're legitimate financial instruments. Weather futures. Last winter was more El Nino than El Nina—or the other way around, I can never remember. Anyway, it didn't go very well. So he moved into frost futures during the spring."

"He bet on whether there'd be a hard frost?" Nana Cole asked. "You can do that?"

"It's not betting. You buy a futures contract and if there's no frost on a particular day it pays off."

"That's betting," my grandmother insisted.

"It's high finance. Anyway, he spent the summer in sunflower seeds and broke even. Now he's pinned his hopes on the fall frost."

"Did he have to pawn his yacht? Is that why you're here?" I asked.

"Do you have any idea how hard it is to be nine months pregnant on a boat? At sea?"

That sounded reasonable. But probably didn't have anything to do with why she was here.

"I'm exhausted," my mother said. "I need to lie down for a nap."

"Where are you planning to do that?" I asked.

"In my room."

"It's my room now."

"Where do you think I'm going to stay?"

"In a hotel."

"You're not being reasonable."

"Henry, you can stay in the other bedroom," my grandmother said.

"The one with all the boxes?"

"There's a bed under there."

"Where will we put the boxes?"

"Put them on the porch and I'll go through them."

This was becoming all too clear. I was expected to carry a room full of boxes down a flight of stairs and onto the porch, all by myself since clearly neither of them could help.

Just then the kettle started to whistle.

———————

OF COURSE, there was no way I was going to move all those boxes on half an Oxy. After I grabbed my stuff from my room —I mean, my mother's room—and put it in the hallway outside my new room, I went into the bathroom downstairs and took an entire 10. Yes, I know, I'm titrating down. But there's nothing to worry about. Given what I used to take, a 10 is nothing.

Then I spent hours moving boxes. Part way through, my mother opened my—uh, her bedroom door and said, "Could you not make so much noise? I'm trying to sleep."

"Seriously?" I said, before thumping loudly down the stairs.

I got most of the boxes onto the porch, some of them were my grandfather's clothes. I couldn't help looking through those. I found a fedora that I instantly fell in love with and a pair of gray flannel slacks from the fifties. He was just my size —at least in the fifties—and I knew the pants would be perfect with a zebra print crop top I had somewhere. I might have loaned it to Vinnie and not gotten it back. I'd have to look.

Speaking of Vinnie, after I got done with the boxes I wanted to call him, so I searched my new room for a phone jack. There was none. Anywhere. I really needed to get my phone back. I made a mental note to put that on my nonexistent to-do list.

I stood there looking at the room. On the one hand, it was a relief to escape my mother's teenage taste: Goodbye home-made French provincial. And on the other, I was now staring at a bedroom full of Mediterranean-style furniture popular two decades before I was born. There was a double bed (an improvement), a nightstand on either side, absurdly gigantic lamps and a wide dresser with a disturbingly large mirror.

There was no desk, which was a bummer since I liked sitting at my mother's desk while I played World of Warcraft III.

Who had lived in this room? I tried to think back to my visits. I'd spent the summer of 1991 in Masons Bay when I was twelve. My mother had wanted to get rid of me, which even then didn't seem surprising. We'd come before that, too. Together. Which never went well. Where did I sleep?

The summer I was here alone, I slept in my mother's room. When we came together, my grandfather was still alive and I slept downstairs. In the room my grandmother now used. The box room was the room my grandparents lived in together. She must have moved downstairs at some point after he died.

Suddenly, my mother was behind me. I jumped. The fedora popped off my head landing on the floor.

"Scaredy-cat."

"Shut up."

"Listen. I need clarity. Did you tell your grandmother you're gay?" She had one hand resting on top of belly like she was some kind of Madonna. Not *Madonna* Madonna. Mother of Christ Madonna. Anyway.

I said, "I did tell her, and she had a stroke and promptly forgot. Remember?"

"You should tell her again."

"Yeah, if you want to kill your mother you should do it yourself."

"I'm sure she'll be fine. Just because one thing happens after another doesn't mean they're connected."

"Yeah, and the fact that you had sex has nothing to do with how you got pregnant."

She sighed heavily. "I'm not saying cause and effect doesn't exist, I'm saying it's rarely the whole story."

I couldn't figure out if that was wise or incredibly stupid or —as is frequently the case with my mother—both.

"Are you going downstairs? I'd like to use the phone in your room."

"What happened to your cell phone? I'm not getting you another one."

I had news for her, she already had. Now I just needed to get it back.

"The police took it. They had a warrant. They searched the house and took my phone and computer."

"Well, you need to get your phone back."

"Yeah. I'll get on that. In the meantime, can I use the phone in your room?"

"Are you going to make a habit of it?"

"I need to call my future roommate."

"Fine, go ahead." And then she waddled away.

I walked down the hallway and into her room. Wow. It looked like a warzone. There were clothes all over the unmade bed—odd because she hadn't changed. The desk was now covered in make-up and moisturizers, hairbrushes and the general contraptions of beauty. I tripped over her empty suitcase, which lay open on the floor. After I followed the cord from the wall, I found the phone buried in the bedsheets.

She'd made a phone call. Presumably to the father of her child. That was a good sign. Maybe that meant she wouldn't be staying. Not that it mattered to me. I was leaving soon.

"Moochie! When will you be here?" Vinnie said, after he picked up. "I have to move out as soon as possible."

I was about to ask if he was serious about moving in together, but I guess I didn't have to.

"Soon," I said. "Very soon. You're not going to believe this, but my mother showed up. She's like thirteen months pregnant."

"You need to leave the minute you get off the phone, darling."

"I know, tell me about it."

"Did you get my money? I'm going to need it for a security deposit."

"Yeah, that's a problem. I think my mother's here because her boyfriend is broke."

"What is this world coming to? Even the rich people are broke. What about you? You must have some money. Collecting all those rewards."

"One. Just one reward. And it's spent."

"How tragic. We're going to need at least two thousand dollars to get a place. I have three hundred. Can you ask your grandmother for the rest? That would be your half and the money you owe me."

"She doesn't want me to leave. She thinks I'll die if I go back to L.A."

"Wow. Pessimistic much?"

"Plus, she says she's leaving me the farm. I think she wants me to be a farmer."

"Fuck that. How soon do you think she might die? She's been ill, hasn't she?"

"She had a stroke."

"Oh, she could have another one at any moment," he said with much too much glee.

"Hold on. Let's not kill off my grandmother quite yet."

"I thought you hated her?"

"I hate a lot of people, that doesn't mean I want them dead."

"Oh my God, you've got a conscience. When did that happen?"

"My grandmother is a lot better. Healthwise. I mean, I wouldn't ask her to carry a bowl of hot soup across a room, but she's improving. Slowly."

"What are we going to do, Moochie? We need money."

Neither of us had a good answer to that question. Which pretty much ended the conversation. At dinner time, I was dispatched to a place in Masons Bay to pick up some of the worst Chinese take-out I've ever had. Ham's Navigator was sitting at the end of the driveway. When I got there, I stopped and cranked my window down. His window glided down.

"I thought you were staying in?"

"I have to pick up take-out from Chin Chang."

He cringed.

"Ah, you've eaten there."

"I have."

"How was Lena Martindale?"

"She wouldn't talk to me. Her husband was there. I'll try again another time."

"My mother's here. That's why we're having Chinese. She has a craving. She's super pregnant."

"That must be nice for you. I bet you can't wait to be a brother."

I glared at him. I'm sure he knew better. "Hey, could you look into her boyfriend for me? His name is David and he's some kind of finance guy. I don't know his last name. Is that enough to go on?"

Ham frowned at me. "Oh, ye of little faith. David Hounsell. He owns an investment firm called Hounsell Income Technologies. H.I.T. He runs a hedge fund rated triple C."

"Wow, how did you find that out?"

"Your mother's name is on a couple of his shell companies. I don't mean to alarm you, but I think the guy's shady and your mother is in it up to her eyeballs."

Crap. Was my mother on the lam? Was she hiding out? This was a terrible place to hide. Her mother's house is probably the first place anyone would look for her. I mean, as long as they didn't know her.

"Are you okay?"

"I'm fine. If you met my mother, you'd know none of this is a surprise."

CHAPTER THIRTEEN

The next morning, I woke up thinking about how I'd ended up in Northern Lower Michigan with my Nana Cole. It had taken some time to put all the pieces together, for various and somewhat obvious reasons.

Basically, I got 5150'd. 5150 is the California law that makes it legal for them to kidnap you and lock you in a psych ward for 72 hours if they think you're a danger to yourself or others. The last bit is the important bit.

After jumping to the conclusion I'd OD'd and calling 911, Vinnie called my mother. Vinnie has a condition that I refer to as Mommy-blindness. His mother, Velma, is fabulous. She's kind, friendly, supportive, and bakes cookies at an alarming rate. There were times when the only food in our apartment was Velma's cookies. She's also always overdressed, wears a ton of makeup, wears her hair sky high, and is the source of Vinnie's bitchy humor. In short, if you didn't know she was a biological woman you'd think she was a drag queen. Which only makes her more fabulous. She's also the reason for Vinnie's Mommy-blindness.

He understands that not everyone's mother is as great as his. But he also doesn't actually believe that a mother might be bad or not very good or even mediocre. In his world, all mommies are good, even when proven otherwise.

Naturally, for him, he assumed that the first thing I'd want to see when I crawled my way out of my presumed overdose would be my mother. He was wrong. Now, I can't say I remember a lot about those three days. They sort of exist in my head like a two-minute movie trailer for a movie no one wants to see. Once I was stable enough to leave the ER, I was sent up to the psych ward. A place that was cold and hard-edged and really, really boring.

A doctor—or more accurately a doctor-trainee, a girl a few years older than I was—whose name I struggled to remember then and now—came in and did an intake interview.

"Were you attempting to kill yourself?"

"No. I was having fun."

"Can you elaborate?"

"I was out in WeHo. Rage. Motherlode. I think I was in Revolver for a while. A guy gave me some pills. I took them."

"Do you know what the pills were?"

"Oxy."

"Dosage?"

"I don't know."

"Do you remember what color the pills were?"

"Pink."

She made a notation on my chart.

"You said *some* pills. Do you remember how many?"

I shook my head. I didn't remember how many pills. I did remember that I might have gotten pills from more than one guy and there might have been more colors involved.

"You had depressive episodes as a teenager. Is that correct?"

"What? Why do you think that?"

"It's in your—" She flipped through my chart, a couple of pages at that point. "Okay, your mother was with you in the emergency room. She provided information she thought you might not."

This was tricky. Dr. Whatever-her-name-was was unlikely to believe me no matter what I said.

Fuck it, I thought. Let's go with the truth.

"My mother was married to this guy named Frank Fetterman from the time I was twelve until I was fifteen. He was an asshole. I wasn't especially cheerful during that period."

"Did you attempt suicide?"

"No."

"Your mother said you threw yourself down a flight of stairs."

"My stepfather pushed me, then told her I did it myself so I could blame him."

She looked at me very closely. I could totally read her mind. I'd been here before. When two people tell different stories about the same thing, the reasonable thing to do is assume the truth lies somewhere between. The problem in those three days was that even if you only believed my mother a little bit, it was really bad for me. And, you know, there was also the whole overdose hoo-ha.

I was released into my mother's care. I remember, before I was released, she and I were sitting on a bench in the hallway, waiting to leave.

"Sweetheart, here's the deal. You can either go into rehab or you can go stay with your Nana Cole in Michigan."

"What?"

"You heard me."

"I don't want to go to rehab." I also didn't want to go to Michigan, but I didn't have an opportunity to say that.

"Then it's settled."

"No."

"I've already packed your things and booked a flight for this evening."

"What?"

"I was pretty confident you'd choose to stay with your grandmother."

"Why would I choose—"

Then a new psychiatrist was there. He looked even younger than Dr. Whatever-her-name-was. He smiled and said, "We're releasing you now. I have a prescription for Zoloft. Also, referrals to psychiatrists in the area accepting—"

"Henry has decided he'll go to Michigan and stay with his grandmother on her farm."

"Ah, well, a change of scene might do you good."

By the next morning I was in Michigan.

Yes, looking back there are all sorts of things I should have said and done to avoid my predicament. In my defense, though, I've dug around the Internet and learned that in addition to some nasty gut issues we will not be discussing, one of the prime features of an accidental overdose is memory loss and mental confusion. In other words, days later I was still not thinking straight.

Anyhoo—that morning I went downstairs for breakfast before my mother woke up. Reilly followed me, gasping he was so excited to be up and awake. It must be pretty cool to be a dog and get all excited just getting out of bed.

In the kitchen, my Nana Cole was at the stove making bacon. After I let Reilly out, I poured myself a cup of coffee and watched her. She wobbled and weaved as she took a fork and tried to flip each piece over. I was sure she was going to flip the pan of grease onto herself or basically fall into it. It was suspenseful, but not in a good way.

"Why don't you let me do that," I said, reaching out for the fork.

"I can do it."

"I know you can do it. I also know you can give yourself third degree burns with bacon grease. Why don't you sit down?"

Grudgingly, she gave me the fork. I flipped a few pieces of bacon before saying, "You remember Ham, the private eye who's following me? He told me some things about Mom's boyfriend."

"Is he following him, too?"

"No. I guess it was part of his investigation into me. It seems like this guy might be kind of shady."

"Uh-huh," she said. "That's your mother's type."

"Well, he's in a lot of financial trouble. Apparently. That's why she's here."

I began laying out the bacon on a paper towel.

"You don't think I fell for it when she said she missed us."

"I wasn't sure. You were being kind of quiet."

"With your mother, if you stay quiet she'll eventually tell you the truth. She won't mean to, she won't even know she's doing it, but she will."

Actually, that was good insight. For a moment, I felt close to my grandmother. Nothing like a common enemy to bring people together. But then, of course, she had to ruin it.

"This Ham person, you're mentioning him a lot. Is he a special friend?"

"God no," I said reflexively. Then I realized what she said meant. I waited a moment, finished laying out the cooked bacon. Then I turned the burner off. "So, you do know I'm gay?"

"No. I don't believe that. I do know that people do terrible things to get drugs. When you finally stop doing drugs you'll be normal. You won't be confused anymore."

"That's not how it works, Nana."

"How would you know? You're still taking drugs, aren't you?"

"I'm titrating down. Taking less and less all the time. That doesn't mean I'm becoming more and more heterosexual."

"It could mean that; you don't know yet."

"So, if I slip an Oxy into your coffee, you'll be attracted to women by lunch time?"

"That's not what I'm saying."

"Actually, it is what you're saying."

My mother walked into the room and our conversation died. She looked at both of us, then said, "Don't stop on my account."

Wisely, Nana Cole changed the subject, "Helena Blinski is having her book club tonight."

"What? Where did you hear something like that?" I asked.

"Jan called me. We think it will be very well attended. They're reading *The Da Vinci Code*."

"It can't be true," I said. "Her husband hasn't been dead for a week. They haven't even had the funeral yet."

"It's very distasteful," Nana Cole said. "But Jan swears she heard from Helena herself. She said that the doctor wouldn't want her to cancel. He'd want her life to be as normal as possible. Somehow, I doubt that very much."

"She was Dr. Blinski's nurse, wasn't she?" My mother asked but then didn't wait for an answer. "I remember her. We were here one time and you broke out in hives. She was very nice."

"She's a whore," Nana Cole said.

"A very nice whore."

"I don't remember any of that," I said.

"How can you not remember that? You were nine or ten, one or the other."

"There's a lot I don't remember about my childhood. I was either very traumatized or very bored."

My mother stared me down and said, "You were bored."

Nana Cole stood up and said, "I'm going to make some pancakes to go with that bacon."

She set about getting the ingredients out of the cupboard while my mother sat there. Finally, she said, "Well, isn't anyone going to ask how I slept? How I am? Anything?"

"You'll tell us if you want us to know," Nana Cole said, without turning around.

"You don't have to tell me," I said. "You slept terribly, and you hate being pregnant."

"I slept wonderfully, and I love being pregnant."

"Liar."

I took a sip of my coffee and she immediately said, "Let me have a sip."

"Get your own coffee. There's plenty."

"I'm not supposed to have coffee. Bad for the baby apparently."

"Then no. You can't have a sip."

"Good for you, Henry," my grandmother said. I hadn't been able to take my eyes off her. Mixing pancakes was harder than I'd have thought. She needed the cane to stand. But she also needed two hands to make the pancakes.

"Said the woman who smoked through three pregnancies," my mother quipped.

"Wait. What?" Seriously, more relatives I was unaware of?

"I lost two babies at birth. Emory, before your mother and Emmett afterward."

"Could you imagine? Emory and Emily! Mother you'd have driven yourself crazy."

"I wouldn't have minded," she said quietly. Then I watched as she wedged her hip against the counter so she could pour pancake batter into the griddle.

"You should start physical therapy again. It would make all that easier." And less stressful for me.

She said, "Mmm-hmm. Did you want to go to that book club?"

"What? Helen Blinski's book club? We're not invited."

"I used to go. Years ago. I stopped going after we read *The Hours*. Disgusting book. You can imagine the discussion it prompted. I have an open invitation. I can go back any time I want."

"Yes," I said. "I think I would like to go."

"Well, then I'm going, too," my mother said.

"We don't all need to go," I said.

"You're right. Mother got the invitation and it'll be mainly a bunch of women drinking wine. Maybe you should stay home."

AN HOUR LATER, with my stomach full of pancakes and rage, I drove down to the end of the driveway stopping to chat with Ham. There must have been steam coming out of my ears, because he looked at me and said, "What?"

"My mother is difficult," I said tersely.

"Most of them are."

"No, most of them aren't. People just think they are. They're wrong."

"Okay. You want to talk about it?"

I thought about it. I could really use a sympathetic ear. Someone to listen to me rave for an hour or so. The thing was, the private eye following me was probably not the right person for that.

"Thanks. I'll take a raincheck."

"Where are you off to?"

"I'm going to the ask the sheriff if I can have my phone back, and then I have to go to the grocery store. My grandmother's making a casserole to bring to Helen Blinski's. Did you hear she's having book club tonight?"

"I did. And it hasn't even been a week since her husband was murdered. Are you going?"

"We are, yes."

"We?"

"Me, my mother and my grandmother."

"That should be interesting."

I frowned for a moment, wondering what he might mean by *interesting*.

"What are you planning to do?" I asked, turning the tables on him.

"Follow you. Where are you doing your shopping?"

"Benson's."

"Okay," he said, as his window rose.

I pulled out onto M-22 and drove to the other side of Masons Bay to the Wyandot County Municipal Center where the sheriff's office was located. Ham passed me long before we got to Duck Pond Road.

The sheriff's office had much more space than it actually needed. There were several empty offices with empty desks sitting outside them. It was like they were planning ahead for a time when crime was skyrocketing in the county. Of course, if you asked me, that time had already come.

I found Detective Rudy Lehmann and, rather than saying 'hello, how are you?' I asked, "Can I have my phone back?"

"Didn't anyone call you?"

"What do you mean? Did something happen to my phone? Did you drop in a toilet?"

Yes, I'd dropped my cell phone into the toilet once. It happens a lot more than you'd think.

"Your phone is fine. You were supposed to get a call on Monday telling you to come and get it."

"Monday? Seriously? It's Wednesday!"

"Sorry. Someone screwed up."

"Can I have my computer, too? Are you finished searching it?"

"Yes, you can have it. No, we aren't finished searching it."

"How does that work?"

"We copied your hard drive onto a Zip disc. So if there is anything incriminating on your computer, we already have it."

"Good to know. So, do you have any other suspects?"

"Working on it."

"You wouldn't like to share?"

"Who do *you* think did it?"

"Robbie, the Pilates instructor. She and Helena are having an affair."

"Are they now."

"You don't think so?"

"I haven't heard that before. Is this that gay radar thing you people supposedly have?"

"Can you get my stuff please?"

He nodded and left his office.

You people. Why was that so offensive? I mean I've been called a lot worse. And it was just two little words. You and people. Neither was offensive on their own, but together they stung. Even though he was probably trying to be nice, or at least not an asshole. But... he kind of *was* an asshole. *You people* meant you weren't like him. You were someone he didn't understand. Someone he couldn't be bothered to understand. He was putting me in the corner. *You people.*

A few minutes later he came back with my phone and my computer. The cell phone was dead, they hadn't taken the charger. It was at home in my new bedroom. I'd have to charge it when I got back. I said a terse thank-you and left.

Benson's is on the other side of Masons Bay, on my way back home. As I drove by the doctor's office, I noticed the crime scene tape had been taken off the front door and it stood open. There was a Chevy pickup truck sitting at the curb with boxes in it. I assumed Nancy Fisher must be packing up. Well, what she could pack up. I'd guess that the medical records had to be kept and stored and guarded—so no one went through them the way Ham had.

I continued on until I got to Benson's County Store, which was in a kind of mini mall with a bank, a pharmacy, a massage place and a car wash.

Oh, funny story—one time I went to Revolver with seven cents in my pocket and got sloppy drunk. A professor of architecture from one of the colleges, I don't remember which, kept buying me drinks and lecturing me on mini malls and the destruction of American culture. By the third drink he had morphed into the ways in which capitalism corrupted, well, everything. I knew he wanted to sleep with me, but I found this such a strange way to do it. Most guys grilled you on what you were willing to put where before you got through the first drink. That way they didn't have to buy you another if they didn't like the way part A would go into part B.

All that said, mini malls in Los Angeles are ugly and to be avoided at all costs. But the mini mall where Bensons Country Store was located was actually kind of charming. It had a rustic feel to it. And, I was fairly certain, it was the only mini mall in Wyandot County. That alone made it refreshing. Mini malls in Los Angeles are everywhere, like acne on a teenager.

Walking into the little store, I grabbed a green plastic basket and took out the list my grandmother had made for me. I needed a pound of ground beef, canned mushrooms, two cans of mushroom soup, sour cream, elbow macaroni, parmesan cheese—the shelf kind that lasts forever and will likely be our primary food source during a zombie apocalypse —potato chips, one onion and garlic salt.

I set about gathering these ingredients, mostly in the canned food aisle. I swung by the meat counter and finally found myself in the produce section. I felt like I should buy something a little healthier, like bananas or an orange. I mean, my mother should actually be eating—

"It's Henry, isn't it?"

The woman was in her thirties, maybe older, very thin, dark-haired with curious eyes. She wore a pair of carpenter pants and a heavy cardigan sweater that she'd obviously made herself. The sweater was rust-colored, looked as though it was misbuttoned but wasn't, and was beginning to fray in several spots.

"Sandy," I said. I'd completely forgotten her last name.

"You came to look at my yurt."

"I did. How is your yurt?"

"It's a yurt."

"Well, nice to—"

"Your aura..."

"Oh God, it's still piss yellow, isn't it?"

"Not all of it. It's a pretty gold in some places. And there are patches of violet."

Oh God, now I'm an Easter basket.

"You've recently had a shock, haven't you?"

"I bet you say that to all the boys."

She just smiled at my skepticism. Well, I certainly wasn't going to admit that she was right. It *was* shocking to find my mother in my grandmother's kitchen.

"Violet means wisdom. It seems that you're beginning to find some. Being a student of life must be paying off."

I have to say, wisdom has never been on my bucket list. I was ready to try ending the conversation again, when she said, "Very sad about Dr. Blinski."

"Were you a patient?"

"Oh no. I don't believe in Western medicine. It's all about pills and profit. Do you know who killed him?"

Apparently, she hadn't heard that people thought it was me.

"No. I'm not really—I'm not—" Okay, well I was actually investigating, so I said, "No. I haven't figured that out yet."

She lowered her voice and said, "He gave people pills they shouldn't have had."

"I've heard that. Yes."

"A friend of mine thinks it was Ronnie Shack who killed him. A territorial dispute."

"Ronnie mainly sells marijuana."

"I know. I'm one of his suppliers. I do a half-acre every summer."

If I remembered correctly, her easement was not agricultural. I could totally bust her. And.... Marijuana was illegal. I could double bust her.

"Isn't it awfully cold up here for that?"

"Oh, I do cuttings. I go down to Florida in the spring and a friend gives them to me."

She needs to be more careful. She just admitted to crossing state lines with a controlled substance. I could be wearing a wire.

"Don't you teach or something?"

"Personal enrichment."

"And what is that again?

"Spiritual centering, yoga, nutrition—what you have in your basket is going to kill you, by the way—breathing, acupressure."

I almost tried to say goodbye again. I really did want to end the conversation. But I couldn't help myself. "So, what do you do for nausea?"

"You can try ginger or peppermint, but I find that acupressure works best."

Crap. She's making a play for me as a client. I said, "Okay, well, thanks..."

"Hold on," she said, grabbing my wrist. "You can do this yourself. Place three fingers just below the crease below your palm. The spot is right there in the center. Using your thumb rub it in a circular pattern for two to three minutes."

I stood there rubbing my wrist.

"Well, I'm running late," she said and pushed her cart away from me, as though I was a weirdo she had to get away from. Which made me wonder, was I really doing acupressure? Or had I just been tricked?

CHAPTER FOURTEEN

When we got to the house on Meadowlark Lane the street was parked up and down. There were enough cars in front of the house that I felt homesick. It was like a glimpse of L.A.

But then I had to park my grandmother's Escalade. Not fun. I'd wanted to drive my car, but my mother turned her nose up at it and refused to get in. Absurdly, she said, "People might see me in that."

I bit my tongue. She looked ridiculous. She wore a pair of black slacks she couldn't snap shut, a white T-shirt stretched to the point of ripping, and a gray cardigan on which she could only button one button.

"Don't you have any maternity clothes?" My grandmother asked before we left the house.

"Why would I buy maternity clothes? I'm not doing this again."

"You should have said something. There are maternity clothes in one of the boxes Henry moved onto the porch. We don't have time to find them right now. We'll get them out tomorrow."

I, on the other hand, looked fabulous. I wore the gray flannel slacks I'd found with a lavender Western-style shirt I'd bought on Melrose Boulevard and paid far too much for, Docs, my bomber jacket and the fedora.

There had been a moment before we left the house, when Nana Cole took in what I was wearing—my grandfather's pants and hat. She seemed to hold her breath for a moment, prompting me to ask, "It's okay that I took them, isn't it?"

"Well, they weren't doing anyone any good in the box," she said. Though I'm not sure she meant it.

I parked a very long way from the house, and we climbed out. Nana Cole got it in her head she was going to carry the casserole herself. That was ridiculous. She'd end up dropping it. I took it away from her and then, before my hands even got warm, my mother took it from me.

"Don't think you're going to take credit for that. Nana Cole made it."

"I don't know why you have such a low opinion of me," she said before she stomped off in front of us.

We walked up the driveway which was full of expensive cars and SUVs. I kept an eye out for Ham sitting in one of them. I didn't see him. We followed a walkway to the front door. I had to walk very slowly, not only did my grandmother take a lot of time, but now I had my mother who was walking like an overweight duck. I know neither of them could help it, but still...

"Is it always this crowded?" I asked.

"No. People come but not like this," Nana Cole said.

The front door was oversized and very grand. Beyond it we could hear a crowd chattering. I rang the doorbell, which earned me a glare from my grandmother.

"It's a party. We can just walk in."

"Really, Henry," my mother chimed in.

As I pushed the door open, I found Ivy Greene on the other side. An attractive woman with translucent skin and dyed red hair, she looked younger than she actually was. Originally, I'd thought late thirties, but her son was my age, so she had to be well into her forties. Like my mother. She wore a pair of elegant black slacks and a filmy black top with silver jewelry.

"Emma, Henry nice to see—is that Emily? My goodness, I haven't seen you in years."

"Oh, um, I don't really—"

"Ivy Greene, we met a couple times at Main Street Café. When you'd visit your mother. I'm a friend of Eva's. Eva Bailey."

"Of course. Ivy Greene. How could I forget?"

Awkward. Did she mean how could she forget a name like Ivy Greene—I certainly couldn't. Or did she mean something else? Eva Bailey was the barmaid at Main Street Café, had something happened? Whatever it was, the look on Ivy's face told me she knew what my mother meant.

Still, she said, "Come in, come in."

We stepped into the foyer which was large and had benches on either side of the door. Over the benches there must have been coat hooks, but you couldn't see them for all the light fall coats. It had been warm during the day, but as soon as the sun went down...

"I brought a casserole," my mother said. Which made it sound like she made it without actually saying she'd made it. I wanted to slap her, but Ivy took care of that.

"Oh Emily, that's so sweet," she lowered her voice. "Book club is always catered. And if there's any meat in there Helena will just throw it out. She's been throwing out casseroles all week."

My mother stood there uncomfortably with the casserole for a moment, and then said, "Henry, maybe you should bring this back to the car."

"The car is a million miles away."

"Oh, you can leave it on the bench," Ivy said, pointing to a spot where another casserole sat. "Try to find a spot to hang up your coats. Can you believe it was nearly eighty last week?"

It must have struck her that was the day Dr. Blinski was murdered, a subject best not broached.

"Well, I hope you've read the book. Helena is bound and determined to discuss it. Usually we can wander off topic, but tonight we really do want to talk about the book."

The last felt like a threat. To be fair, Ivy knew I liked to ask questions about murder. I'd asked her enough. With a jaunty smile, she walked away.

My mother set the casserole down next to the other one. We took our coats off, and since there were no open hooks, laid them on the bench next to the casseroles. I said a prayer that neither my fedora nor my bomber jacket picked up any disgusting smells from the casserole we'd brought. Probably a hopeless cause.

Nana Cole said, "Your mother's right, Henry. You should take that casserole out to the car."

"Uh—I already said no."

"Otherwise, we'll have to throw it away."

I shrugged. It didn't bother me at all that we'd be throwing it away. The idea of eating it made me sick. I said, "I don't care."

"That's your problem, Henry. You never care," she said in a very sharp tone, then walked off. My mother raised an eyebrow at me and followed her.

What the—what did she mean by that? I *cared*. I cared about lots of things. Sometimes I even cared about people. Sometimes I cared about her—against my better judgment. I didn't care about a casserole. Why would I care about that?

Grumpy now, I walked into the living room. I was subtly pressing my thumb into my wrist making clockwise circles hoping to settle my stomach. In addition to driving over here with that casserole in the car, it was time for my next half 10. I wanted to find the bathroom so I could have a moment alone to take it. But first, it seemed like a good idea to check everything out.

The living room was very large and yet looked very small. There were probably thirty, forty people crammed in like sardines and making an incredible noise. Half of them had brand-new, obviously unread copies of *The Da Vinci Code* clutched in one hand, prominently displayed.

I could see that Bev and Barbara standing with Jan next to the overflowing buffet table, which had two caterers in black-and-white standing guard so people didn't start to eat. I noticed Olly Hanson handing out business cards, Opal belligerently hovering in a corner (she saw me and glowered), and Nancy Fisher, there with a younger pregnant woman who was probably her daughter.

Nearby, at the center of a large group, was Helena Blinski herself. She was a beautiful woman just beyond fifty. She had dark, wavy hair expertly cut. It hung to her shoulders, and it looked as though she might flip it back at any moment and laugh. Of course, she didn't. She was a widow. Widows could smile enigmatically but not laugh. A black shawl was draped across her chest from one shoulder to the other. I couldn't see what else she was wearing. There were too many people.

My mother took my grandmother's arm to stabilize her. That earned a nasty slap on the hand.

"What do you think you're doing?"

"I don't want you getting knocked over."

Nana looked her up and down, and said, "We'll see who gets knocked over first." And with that she launched herself into the crowd, and even with the din I heard a few people saying "Ouch" as she stomped by.

My mother looked at me, shrugged, then followed.

I decided it was time to go to the bathroom. I stepped back into the foyer and turned right. There was the staircase to the second floor and a hallway that led down to the kitchen. There must have been a guest bathroom beneath the stairs, because there was a line of about six women. No. I was not getting in that line.

Slipping up the stairs quietly, I reached the second floor and began looking for another bathroom. I opened doors until I found what was obviously the master bedroom, a grand four-poster and its own balcony. I guessed that it might have its own bathroom. I found the walk-in closet first, packed to the brim. And then, next to it, the master bath. Blissfully empty.

I stepped in, closed the door, and took off my shoes. I pulled out my travel stash—just a couple pills in case of emergency, and picked out the meager half 10 I was going to take. Titrating down was a sad affair. I was going to miss drugs. They did such a good job of taking the edge off. And my life had a lot of edges. The things that happened to me in the last few months would have hurt so much more if I hadn't had my friendly opioids to help me through. I had no idea what I'd do without them.

I might have to get a best friend.

I mean, Vinnie was a *good* friend—when he didn't have a boyfriend. And Opal was, well, at best a frenemy. An *actual* friend would have fought her way through the crowd the minute she saw me. But she didn't. She just glowered.

And that was pretty much it. If I wasn't going to do drugs, I would have to make more friends. The kind who didn't do drugs. Oh my God, that didn't leave many options.

Filling my palm with water, I took my lonely half 10. Then I put my stash back in my shoe and slipped the shoe back on.

Then I did what I always do in a stranger's bathroom: I looked through the medicine cabinet. The bathroom was fabulous, of course. I'd been so intent on my half pill that I'd barely noticed. Now, I saw that the medicine cabinet was mirrored and double-doored, with large mirrors on both sides that continued along the wall.

I stopped and spent a little time on my hair. The hat had messed it up. A bit. Not that the style wasn't a little 'messy,' it just had to be the right mess. That fresh 'I just rolled out of bed' look really works for me. Just saying.

Then I opened the medicine cabinet and took inventory. *Holy crap she had a lot of drugs.* Well, she was married to a doctor after all. A doctor who was a bit loose with the prescription pad. She had a lot of Oxy and Vicodin and Diazepam and Viagra—that probably wasn't Helena's—and a whole bunch of less interesting drugs. High blood pressure meds, cholesterol meds, antacids and on and on... It was a virtual pharmacy—not dissimilar to the one Dr. Blinski had at his office.

With great difficulty, I resisted the temptation to fill my pockets. Okay, I did take a couple of Oxy. Ten. Definitely not enough to be noticed. I left the bathroom, walked through the bedroom and into the hallway. There was Ham.

"What are you doing up here?"

I didn't bother with an answer and got right to the point. "Did you look through the medicine cabinet? It's chock full."

"A doctor lived here. That can't be surprising."

"Except," I said, not completely sure what I was about to say. "Well, it doesn't make sense. I mean, yeah, a doctor lived here. So there are a lot of drugs. And... if Helena wanted to kill him, she could have easily overdosed him. I don't think anyone would have looked too closely. And nobody could be sure he didn't do it to himself, if they did."

"Did you really think she killed him?"

"It was a working theory."

Mostly because she wanted the killer to be me. I'd been thinking she had someone kill her husband for her. But maybe someone she knew, someone she cared about killed him without asking. Like, *Surprise! Happy birthday, I killed your husband for you!*

"Do you know when Helena's birthday is?"

"No. I don't." He looked confused but didn't ask why I'd asked.

"Do you think the killer is downstairs?" I asked.

"That's a possibility."

"It doesn't seem very smart, though."

"Maybe they love books and just couldn't resist," he said.

I rolled my eyes at him and went back downstairs. Somehow it seemed even more crowded. Not to worry, I'd navigated Rage on a Saturday night with a drink in each hand; I could handle a book club. Even one where most of the people there just wanted to gawk at the brand-spanking new widow.

I noticed that people were holding plastic glasses, which meant alcohol was being served somewhere. It took a moment, but I eventually saw the wine table on the opposite side of the room from the buffet table. It was at that point that I realized most of the actual furniture in this room had been removed. Helena must have realized people would show up in droves and she'd made room for them.

What kind of person loses their husband and less than a week later has a party? Wait, that was a dumb question. Most people had a party shorty after someone died. They just didn't call it book club, they called it a wake. This kind of was a wake. Most of the people were wearing black.

I fought my way across the room to the wine table. And when I say fought, I mean it. I had to nudge, squish, rub up against, gently push, and weasel my way across the room. I was officially now a deviant. The kind who likes to press up against strangers. Not that I enjoyed it, it was kind of disgusting.

The wine made it worthwhile, though. The cater waiter poured me a glass and told me it was from Masons Bay Cellars. Not that I, or anyone else there, cared. It was free.

I decided to hover near the table so I could get a second glass. This evening would be made so much better by a slight buzz. I eased my way over to the wall and was looking over the crowd trying to find my mother and grandmother, when Sue Langtree stepped on my toe.

"Ouch, that really hurt!"

"I'm so sorry," she said in the most insincere way possible.

Sue Langtree was in her early seventies, white hair, pink skin and very determined facial features. She was the choir director at my grandmother's church. She was also a murderer.

She'd killed Reverend Hessel at the start of summer and managed to pin it on a teenage rapist named Donny Hyslip. I wasn't losing a lot of sleep over Donny, but it did bother me that Sue was literally getting away with murder.

"I have to ask a very obvious question," she said. "Did you read the book?"

"I did actually."

"Really? You don't strike me as the type who reads."

She was right. The only reason I'd read it was that it was in the giftshop when Nana Cole was in the hospital recovering from her stroke. She was pretty nonverbal at the time, and I had to do something. I didn't tell Sue any of that.

"You don't strike me as the type to murder people," I said, quietly.

"What? You'll have to speak up. It's so loud in here."

Well, I wasn't going to shout that. I asked, loudly, "Did you like the book?"

"Yes. My favorite character was the albino priest who went around killing people."

She'd heard exactly what I'd said.

"What did you think of the book?" she asked.

"I thought it was hysterical."

"It's not supposed to be funny. It's a thriller."

"It's a thriller about a symbologist. Seriously? I don't believe that's a real thing. And if it is a real thing it would be incredibly boring."

"I thought it was absolutely the most exciting book I've ever read. I certainly didn't believe a word of it, but that's why it's called fiction."

"Speaking of fiction, did you hear that Donny Hyslip has an alibi?"

"I did. Some little slut says she was with him when Reverend Hessel was killed. Big deal."

"It will be a big deal if they believe her."

"I'm not worried," she sipped her wine. "Bekah's doing well. Thank you for asking."

"I'm glad your granddaughter is doing well."

"She's thinking of finishing high school early and starting college."

"Good for her."

Though it sounded like small talk, it wasn't. Sue was reminding me that if she got arrested for murder her granddaughter could get hurt in the process. Sue murdered someone and should go to prison. Donny Hyslip raped someone, and he should go to prison, too. The thing was, Donny would never go to prison for raping Bekah Springer. The crime had never been reported and there was no actual evidence. It was all just a big mess and, somehow, I'd ended up the position to worry about what was and wasn't justice.

I could tell Detective Lehmann what I knew, and then Sue would go to prison and Donny would be free. Or I could keep my mouth shut and Donny would go to prison while Sue remained free.

It was not the kind of decision I enjoyed. I much preferred deciding which beer bust to attend on a Sunday afternoon and what to wear to garner the most attention. *What is justice?* was simply above my pay grade.

"Oh, I see a friend. You'll have to excuse me," Sue said, before she walked off, managing to step on my toes yet again.

"Ouch!"

CHAPTER FIFTEEN

"Cheryl Ann talks about you all the time," Dolores said.

I'd gotten another glass of wine and had been attempting to cross the room so I could get closer to Helena Blinski—the whole point of coming to book club—but then I got waylaid by Dolores Abbott.

"I gather there's some kind of love triangle between that awful girl, Opal, and you and my Cheryl Ann," she said, while aiming a death stare across the room toward Opal.

"No, there isn't."

"So you're *not* dating Opal?"

"God, no." I practically shivered in disgust.

"Oh, Cheryl Ann will be so pleased."

She would be. She wanted to be dating Opal herself. Of course, her mother was completely unwilling to see that.

"Now, I've heard the rumors about you killing Dr. Blinski. I don't believe them for a minute. Of course, you and Cheryl Ann can't *officially* start dating until you've cleared that up. Don't want my daughter dating a convicted felon, now do I? Not even a wrongly convicted one."

I smiled at her. The temptation to say, 'Yes, I killed Dr. Blinski,' to make her go way was very strong.

"Don't think that means you can't call her, though. She'd love to hear from you."

I excused myself and continued making my way across the room. "Excuse me...sorry... excuse me."

About five feet away from Helen Blinski and her minions, Bev stood with Barbara. Barbara was a bit older than Bev and had just lost her grandson in Iraq. While she didn't exactly look happy, she did look happier than I'd seen her in a long time. I don't know why. She wasn't the type to take pleasure in other people's grief—though from where I stood it didn't look like Helena was grieving much.

"I see your mother's here," Bev said. "You must be glad to see her."

I ignored that. Bev knew better.

"Is that Robbie the Pilates instructor?" I asked, meaning the small but well-muscled woman standing next to Helena. She was in her mid-thirties with cropped hair, wearing a black tank top and out-of-style black jeans.

"It is," Bev said uncomfortably.

That was weird. *I'd have to figure that out later*, I thought, just as the crowd shifted a little and I saw that Robbie was wearing a medical boot, like the one I'd been given after I sprained my ankle. That was interesting. When had she injured herself? Could she have done it climbing in and out of Dr. Blinski's window? Or had it happened before? And how would I figure that out?

"Do you know what she's having?" Barbara asked.

"What who's having?"

"Your mother. Do you what she's having?"

"A baby."

"Boy or girl?"

"No clue. I'm not sure she believes in prenatal care."

Bev shook her head at Barbara, and said, "He's just being silly."

Actually, I wasn't, but I let it pass.

"What's the deal with Robbie's foot?" I asked.

"I think she stepped in a rabbit hole while hiking up in Sleeping Bear," Bev said.

"How did she manage that?" Barbara asked. "A rabbit wouldn't make its home in the middle of a path."

"She must have left the beaten path," Bev said. They both smiled as though that meant something. What, I had no idea. I was too busy wondering if Robbie hurt herself the day Dr. Blinski was killed. If she did it while... well, that would explain why Helena hired Ham to prove that I'd killed the doctor. She was protecting Robbie.

"Do you know when that happened?"

"Oh gosh," Bev said. "It might have been last Tuesday. Wednesday, maybe."

"Definitely before the doctor was killed," Barbara said. "I heard she hasn't left Helena's side since it happened."

"Sweet," Bev said. Then made an effort to change the subject. "Do you know anything about tonight's book, Henry?"

"Yes. *The Da Vinci Code*. I read it."

"Oh, did you like it?"

"It was stupid. I have a degree in communications, and I can't find a job. How does someone get a job with a degree in symbology?"

"I think he's a professor," Bev said.

"Yeah, but why would anyone take a class in symbology? Is it an elective you need for graduation? I mean, I never heard of it, and we had some weird classes. I took this one, called The Comic Spirit. Nowhere near as fun as it sounded."

"He was a professor at Harvard, they might have different—"

"And all those puzzles he had to solve? I mean, what was that about? At first they were kind of hard, but I got the hang of it easily enough so the last fifty pages I was screaming,

'Apple! Apple!' and the guy, the symbologist, couldn't figure it out."

"Oh," Barbara said. "I haven't actually finished—"

"Sorry, I didn't mean..."

Someone was clinking something—obviously not a plastic glass. A plate on the buffet? The crowd quieted down. Everyone turned to look at Helena. She smiled at us.

"I want to thank you all for coming. Your support in these trying times is so important. Your kindness, not only to me, but to my dear Caspar. The wonderful things you've all said... he'd be so proud. He was a simple country doctor and you all meant so much to him. So very much. I also want to tell you that it was actually Caspar who suggested *The Da Vinci Code*. He adored the book and I hope you all did too."

Okay, I was going to have to start keeping my mouth shut about the book. Otherwise, I'd be insulting the hostess. Who, awkwardly, seemed to be staring right at me.

"The book starts with a murder, of course. Something we can all identify with, unfortunately. I have to say it's possible, even likely, that the murderer is in this room."

Still staring at me. Now other people were too.

"If any of you know anything that would help us catch the killer, please tell Detective Lehmann, who has kindly agreed to be here tonight."

Was this some kind of trap? Was she trying to catch the killer? That didn't make sense, though. I was sure she knew who did it. So, was she trying to catch me?

"We're going to open the buffet now. And I want to remind you all, as Caspar reminded me every day: live, laugh, and love."

Everyone there immediately rushed the buffet table. I did not. Not because I wasn't hungry, now that my stomach had settled I was *very* hungry. No, I stood there thinking, *Is she full of it?* Dr. Blinski didn't seem like the kind to say 'live, laugh, and love' to his wife every day. I felt like she was making that up so we wouldn't think about the fact that her lesbian lover was standing next to her. Now, Robbie the Pilates instructor, *she* might tell Helena to live, laugh, and love every day. That made sense to me.

Bev and Barbara had gone to the buffet with Jan, and I found myself staring at Nancy Fisher, her daughter and a young man a little older than I am. He looked familiar, but I couldn't place him. I stepped over and said, "Hi, Nancy. How are you?"

"Fine," she said. Reluctantly, she introduced me to her daughter, "This is my daughter, Jemma. And my nephew Elbert."

Elbert? Seriously? That's what I thought. What I said was, "Nice to meet you."

He was a sullen looking guy, clearly unhappy. Then I remembered it was his sister who died from a bee sting just a little while ago. Okay, he had a right to be sullen. Especially if he liked her.

I couldn't shake the feeling I'd seen him before. But then, maybe I'd been here too long. Everyone was starting to look like someone I knew—or was potentially related to.

I asked the question you're supposed to ask at book club: "Did you read the book?"

"I read a couple chapters," Elbert said.

"What did you think?"

"There were a lot of words. Like, too many."

I had to assume he preferred picture books. Or comics.

"We hadn't really been planning on coming," Nancy said. "But then, it kind of feels like a wake, don't you think?"

"It does kind of, yes." I turned to Jemma and Elbert and asked, "Did you both know Dr. Blinski."

"Kind of," Jemma said. "He was our doctor."

"So you saw him regularly?"

"From the time we were kids," Jemma said. Her cousin just looked angry.

"Do you know what's going to happen to the doctor's practice?" I asked Nancy.

"Are you a doctor?"

"Of course not."

"Then I'd say it's none of your business."

I took that to mean Helena would be selling it. I mean, why would she keep it?

Nancy looked at her daughter and nephew, and said, "Why don't you kids get in line for the food." Jemma didn't need to be told twice; she was off like a shot. Elbert lingered.

Nancy looked like she might walk away from me, so I asked, "What does it mean to sell a practice, exactly? What would you be selling?"

"The patient list, the house, the supplies, the good will."

"And you'd stay with the practice?"

"I have no idea. And it's still none of your business."

"Have you spent a lot of time there this week?"

"I haven't been back since the doctor was murdered. I don't think I could bear it." She gave me a hard stare. "Why are you asking so many questions?"

"I think I asked like three questions and maybe a few follow-ups." I had no idea, but I wanted to minimize the whole thing. Act like I was just being social, making small talk.

"Look, I'm sorry I thought you killed Dr. Blinski. It was an honest mistake. You don't have to try and turn it around on me. You of all people know I didn't do anything. You were there. You saw me before you went into his office."

"I don't think you had anything to do with it. But... I drove by the other day and there was a truck out front with boxes in it. It looked like someone was packing up. I thought it might be you."

"It wasn't me. And I don't know anything about that. Are you sure the boxes were from your office? Couldn't they have been, I don't know, someone moving? There's an apartment upstairs."

Behind me, I heard my mother's laugh. Then someone asked her, "What are you having?"

She said, "A baby."

I turned and stared at her. That was *my* joke. The idea that my mother and I might be more alike than I wanted to admit hit me like a bucket of cold water in the face. No, no, no, we were nothing alike! She was manipulative, shallow, impulsive and irresponsible. And, while I aspire to be all of those things I rarely succeed.

She saw me looking at her, and said, "What?"

"Nothing."

I turned back to Nancy Fisher, but she was gone. Elbert was still standing there. Glancing at the buffet, I considered trying to force my way through but decided to wait. There was a lot of food. I could bide my time.

"Leave my aunt alone."

"What? I didn't... I don't know what you mean."

"You tried to say she was in the doctor's office when she wasn't. You need to leave her alone."

"I didn't mean to say she did anything wrong. It's logical to think that if the office was being boxed up, she'd be the one doing that—"

I shut up because of the way he was staring at me. He looked like he wanted to tell me to leave his aunt alone again, but, really, he didn't have to. I'd gotten the message loud and clear. I'd be leaving her alone. He turned and walked away.

Okay, that was creepy. Very creepy. The thing is, I'd have been leaving his aunt alone anyway. I was pretty sure her accusing me of murder was an honest mistake. One she'd just apologized for. I didn't think she'd killed the doctor. He'd just died right before I fell on him. He was that warm. Obviously, she didn't stab him. She'd have been covered in blood. And she had no reason to kill him that I knew of. It was entirely possible, no, probable she'd be losing her job. She had the opposite of a motive.

Then Rudy Lehmann walked up. A blonde in a tiny black dress clung to his arm as though death—or reading—was contagious. She wore a lot of makeup and a stunned expression.

"Henry Milch, this is my wife, Gloria."

Honestly, she looked like a hooker, and I wondered if this was one of those stereotypical cop/prostitute marriages.

"Hi Gloria, nice to meet you."

I'd had no idea he was married. I mean, I'd had no idea he wasn't married. All I really knew was that his clothes were always wrinkled. Otherwise, I didn't think about him much.

"Gloria hates crowds," he said.

"I do. There's just so many people," she said, softly. "I think I must have been stomped to death in a previous life."

"Just stay close, sweetie, and you'll be fine."

He was blushing when he turned back to me. "The sheriff wants me to remind you that you shouldn't leave town."

"For how long? I have an opportunity to get an apartment in West Hollywood."

Okay, so we definitely couldn't afford an apartment in West Hollywood, but I didn't want to say the Hollywood flats or East Hollywood, which were gross—or even worse, Koreatown.

"It's going to take as long as it takes."

"This seems more like a wake than a book club," Gloria said. "Have you heard when the funeral is?"

"No, I haven't," I said.

It was obvious Lehmann was uncomfortable talking to me in front of his wife, and it seemed like he was about to suggest they get some food or, whatever, so they could walk off. I decided to jump in...

"So, hypothetically, if person A was, for example, a high school girl who was raped by person B, a high school boy, and then person A found out she was in trouble and persons C and

D helped her resolve that trouble, and then person E found out about what happened—"

Detective Lehmann, who'd been looking confused, asked, "Are you going to use the entire alphabet?"

"No, I'm done. I mean, yes. Just one more letter. Anyway, oh crap, where was I?"

"Person E," Gloria said.

"Thank you. So, hypothetically, if person E found out about persons C and D helping to get person A out of trouble and then blackmailed persons C and D causing person C to kill person E, and then plant evidence so that person B was arrested for the crime—"

"Is there an actual question here?"

"Let's say person F knows all about this. What should person F do?"

"Is this the plot to *The Da Vinci Code*? Because I didn't read the book."

"No, honey," Gloria said. "It's a moral dilemma. Do you let the rapist go free so that you can punish the murderer, or do you let the murderer go free so you can punish the rapist?"

"Wow," I said, "you actually followed that."

"I teach algebra."

Okay, that was a surprise.

"I don't understand why you can't punish them both," Detective Lehmann said.

"I'm guessing, I mean hypothetically, there's very little evidence of rape and a rape trial is a horrible thing for a teenage girl. It's very possible she's the one who'd end up getting punished and the boy will still go free."

"It's still a matter for the sheriff's office. Person F needs to come in and talk about this."

Gloria frowned at her husband. "What person F needs to think about is whether person C will kill again, because it's very likely that person B *will* rape again. So, if you let person

C go no one gets hurt. If you let person B go another woman will get raped."

"Oh, thank you," I said. That was all suddenly much clearer in a very foggy way. I should leave things as they were.

"Honey, I think we should go get some food," Detective Lehmann said in a pointed way.

"It was so nice to meet you," Gloria said. "Don't worry, you'll make the right decision."

And then they walked off. I wondered if it was time for me to get something to eat. It looked like people had slowed down but now they were just standing, three deep, munching in front of the food. I was deciding on ways I could cut through the crowd, when I heard, "I knew you'd come if I had book club."

I turned and there was Helena Blinski, hating me.

"If you wanted to talk to me, you could have called me on the phone or asked me over or just about anything that didn't require catering."

She smiled at me as though I was an idiot. Maybe she didn't want to call me because there'd be a record of that. But why wouldn't she want anyone to know—

"So, did you kill my husband?"

"No."

"That's not what Nancy Fisher says."

"Newsflash. She was wrong and she's admitted it."

"Has she?" That smile again. "You're the only one who could have done it."

"Someone climbed in the window."

"In broad daylight? In Masons Bay? It's a small town, someone would have noticed that."

"It's a small town, maybe there was no one around to notice it?"

"Sheriff Crocker assures me you'll be arrested soon."

"Great. I have something to look forward to."

With a thin, widow's smile, she turned and wafted off, saying, "Lizbeth! How did you like the book?"

Crap, I'd thought I was in the clear. Would the sheriff really arrest me without evidence? Would he make some up? Would Detective Lehmann go for that? He seemed a lot more interested in justice than the sheriff. He wouldn't just stand by while—oh, food.

The crowd had shifted and I could see through to the buffet. Between my Nana Cole on one side chatting with Reverend Wilkie, and my mother on the other flirting with a guy just over thirty who was probably the only truly attractive guy there—not to mention nearly a dozen other people nibbling and chatting—I caught sight of a gigantic wheel of baked brie. It had to be a foot and a half across. People had been digging at it. The crust was perfectly brown and there was some kind of red jam oozing out over the melting cheese. I had to have some. All I had to do was squeeze in between my family and a bevy of random strangers.

I moved quickly and stealthily, and then there I was standing right next to the buffet. Still getting jostled and bumped, but I was there. Surrounding the brie were piles of wafer-style crackers. I picked one up, then looked around for a knife to spread the cheese. There didn't seem to be one anywhere. I kept looking even as I continued to be bumped and jostled. At one point someone elbowed me in the back, hard, and I nearly fell into the cheese. Of course, when I looked behind me there wasn't—

Screw it. I turned back and dipped a cracker directly into the cheese. Of course, it broke. I popped one half into my mouth. Raspberry. The jam was raspberry. Delicious. Then I tried to carefully pick the other half of the cracker out of the cheese, while managing to get at least some of the gooey cheese onto the cracker.

"Oh my God, Henry!" my mother screamed behind me.

"Sorry. I know it's gross, but I can't find a knife," I said, assuming she was calling me on my lack of manners.

To be fair, I was really hungry. But then I looked over my shoulder and saw that she was pale and looked terribly frightened. *Was she about to have her baby?*

"Henry there's a knife in your back."

As it turns out, that's where the cheese knife went.

CHAPTER SIXTEEN

People began screaming. Okay, maybe it was just me. Long, inarticulate screams, followed a few moments later by, "Take it out! Take it out!"

I turned and looked at the people around me. They'd backed up so that I was now standing in the only empty spot in the room. And then Detective Lehmann was there saying, "You can't take the knife out, that's very dangerous. Gloria is calling an ambulance right now."

I could feel blood leaking into my underwear and then down my leg. Oh God, I thought, *I've ruined another fabulous outfit!*

Detective Lehmann was saying something.

"What?"

"I said, 'Do you feel dizzy at all?'"

"No," I said, as I slumped to my knees. "Well, maybe yes."

He got on the floor next to me. "Whatever you do, don't faint onto the knife. Okay? Faint forward."

"Yeah, sure."

And then, suddenly, the pain kicked in and I felt... well, like I'd been stabbed in the back.

"What on earth is happening?" Helena Blinski asked, as she broke through the crowd.

"Someone has stabbed Henry Milch," Detective Lehmann said.

"Well, that's poetic justice. I know he stabbed my Casper. He's just getting what he deserves—oh, but he's bleeding on my rug! Could we put towels down? Quickly! I'm never going to get that stain out."

"Oh shut up, Helena!" That was my Nana Cole, though I couldn't see her. Couldn't lift my woozy head up to look at her.

"He didn't kill your husband and your rug is the last thing you should be worried about! Whore."

"How dare you call me that in my own house!"

There was a brief pause before I heard my mother, "Don't you raise your hand to my mother! She's an old lady—and you *are* a whore!"

"I'm a whore? Emily Cole, do you have *any* legitimate children?"

"No, I don't! And proud of it!"

At that point, I prayed I was hallucinating from blood loss. As I carefully fainted forward, I hoped the ambulance would be quiet.

The next forty-eight hours are a fuzzy mess. I remember things here and there, but long stretches are pretty much gone. Apparently, I lost a lot of blood—or at least enough to be given a transfusion. I woke up in the emergency room, lying on my stomach. I looked over my shoulder and saw a bag of blood hanging there. Presumably, I had an IV somewhere and the blood was flowing into me. I mean, I didn't think it was there to be decorative.

Dr. Edward Stewart bent over to look me in the face. Edward, who was quite possibly the most beautiful man I'd ever—oh God, I shouldn't think that way. Our one almost-date had ended badly when he figured out I had a little Oxy problem. He made it clear he didn't date addicts. *Rude*, I thought. Accurate, but still rude.

When he saw my eyes were open, he said, "You know, if you want to see me there are other ways to make it happen."

That was weird. I was sure he didn't *want* to see me. Now it seemed like he was flirting. If I didn't have a knife sticking out of my back, I might have flirted back.

"I'm going to live, right?"

"You know that you've been stabbed?"

"Uh-huh."

"The knife, a cheese knife? has gone in about two and half possibly three inches. It may be preventing more intense bleeding. We're concerned that things will get significantly worse when we take the knife out. For that reason, we'll be doing it in an operating room."

"I'm not—it feels like I've been bleeding a lot, but you think it could get worse?"

"Whoever stabbed you moved the knife around, possibly on purpose, so the wound itself is about twice the size of the knife. That's why there's a lot of superficial bleeding."

Superficial? Wow, even my bleeding is shallow.

"I need to take care of my other patients. You're going to be okay, though. The surgeon is here and he's scrubbing in. You're not even going to remember most of this."

"I won't forget you. I couldn't."

Then he was gone; or I was. I'm not sure which.

The next thing I remember is waking up in a room with a man who was snoring terribly. I was lying on my back, thank God. The minute someone sticks a knife in your back and everyone says 'Don't roll over' that's the only thing in the world you want to do.

Nana Cole and my mother were sleeping in chairs next to my bed. At first I thought that was sweet, but then I remembered neither of them could drive so they probably just got stuck at the hospital. I fully expected they'd wake up and demand I drive them home. I fell back to sleep and didn't wake up for a couple of hours.

Then I was woken by, "Oh Mother, you can't be serious. Bush knows what he's doing? That's a joke. And what I don't understand is why you trust these people so much. I've been a Democrat since I could vote, and believe me, I don't trust them."

"How can you vote for people you don't trust?"

"Simple. It's the lesser of two evils."

"That's a terrible choice."

"Yes. You're right. But it's the one we always seem to have to make, because in a choice between a little bit evil and a lot evil, I just don't understand why people keep choosing a lot evil."

"You really think we'd be better off if we'd elected Clinton's toady Gore?"

"We did elect Gore. The Electoral College *selected* Bush. It *is* different. Something I'm sure you'd be pissed off about if things had gone the other way. And I do think we'd be better off. I think Al Gore would have paid attention to our intelligence if he'd been in office."

"Now who's trusting them too much?"

I moaned. Nothing hurt, I just couldn't stand listening to them. My mother leaned over me as best she could with her belly in the way. "Do you need something Henry? Water?"

"Pain."

"I'll check and see when you can have more pain medication."

My mother left the room, which left me alone with Nana Cole. I allowed my head to fall in her direction. I was expecting a look of sympathy, perhaps a gentle smile. But the look she was giving me... Ouch. She knew I wasn't in pain. She knew I was faking. *How does she know things like that?*

I turned away, hoping she'd be gone soon. And, in a way,

she was. The nurse came in and gave me another shot of morphine and, well, bye-bye...

A few hours later... I think. It might have been minutes. Or the next day. I don't know. Anyway...

"You're going to have to tell me what's going on sooner or later," I heard my grandmother saying. "You've only ever come home when something was wrong. It's best you just tell me. Your boyfriend threw you out, didn't he? Doesn't want kids, I suppose."

"David's not like that. He's a wonderful man."

"A wonderful man who's gotten you pregnant and won't marry you."

"I never said he wouldn't marry me."

"So, when's the wedding?"

"Things are complicated at the moment."

"That's what you always say."

"Well, this time it is. Can we drop it? We should be worrying about Henry."

"The doctor said he should be just fine. They got everything sewn back together. There's nothing to worry about."

"Except he's still taking pills."

"He says he's tapering off." The doubt she managed to squeeze into such a short sentence was brutal.

"This isn't going to help," my mother said.

"No, I don't imagine it will."

They were quiet a moment. Or maybe I fell back to sleep for a bit. Then my grandmother said, "You're always dropping your problems on my doorstep."

"You always fix them. That's why I keep doing it."

At some point, Bev and Barbara came and got my mother and grandmother and brought them home. I don't really remember that, though I heard about it after the fact. They just stopped being there every time I woke up.

That next afternoon, Detective Lehmann came to see me. My roommate was watching the TV, some news program droning on and on about the second anniversary of 9/11. It was far too soon to be reminding us about that. We'd barely had time to forget.

"How are you feeling?" Detective Lehmann asked.

They'd taken out the IV and started managing my pain with pills. It was about twenty minutes after I'd been given a Vicodin, at least a 20. On an empty stomach no less. I was feeling nothing but bliss. Really, I needed to get stabbed more often.

"I said, how are you feeling," he repeated.

"Fabulous."

"Then I'd like to ask you a few questions."

"As long as they're not mathematical, I think we'll be fine," I joked.

He frowned at me, then asked, "You didn't see who stabbed you?"

"I did not. They were behind me." Even as high as I was, something seemed odd. "Didn't my mother see them? My grandmother? They were both there."

"No one saw who stabbed you."

"It was a room full of people, I mean, really full."

"And people were drinking and eating and talking. And there weren't a lot of good sight lines."

"You think they're going to get away with stabbing me?"

"What about person ABCD? Were they there?"

"I don't want to say."

"That means they were, otherwise you'd just say no."

"No?" I said weakly.

"I know your whole 'hypothetical' question had something to do with Donny Hyslip. You're telling me he didn't kill Reverend Hessel but he did rape someone. Who did he rape?"

"I don't want to say."

"Bekah Springer is the girl who turned him in. I remember you guessing her name before I even said it. She's the girl, isn't she?"

"Can I plead the fifth?"

"Did you rape her?"

"No, of course not."

"Then I don't think you can plead the fifth. The fifth amendment has to do with self-incrimination. You can't take the fifth when I ask questions about crimes you're not involved in."

"Okay. Do I have to answer your questions?"

"Well, no, you don't."

"I'm not answering any more questions."

"I'm trying to find out who stabbed you. And I have a feeling it might be the same person who killed Reverend Hessel."

"It makes sense that it might be the same person who killed *Dr. Blinski*. We were both stabbed."

"In all three cases the weapon was one of convenience. I think I'm looking for one person rather than two."

"No, you're not. The person who killed Reverend Hessel couldn't have climbed through the window."

"Really? That's how you want to play this? Like it's twenty questions? Do I have to ask, 'Are they bigger than a bread box?'"

"Yes. They are."

"I wasn't—it was a—murderers are *always* bigger than bread boxes. It wasn't a serious question. Just tell me who killed Reverend Hessel."

I kept my mouth shut.

"I have half a mind to stab you myself."

"That wouldn't be a good idea, the nurse saw you come in here."

"It's also a bad idea because it's wrong. Do you understand right and wrong?"

"Sometimes."

I was afraid I was going to have to faint again to make him go away, but he left after that. I was exhausted. I couldn't understand why simply talking to someone was taking so much out of me.

Later, I think, Opal showed up. Her hair was beginning to fade. She looked more like she had a kitchen floor on her head than a checkerboard.

"You look okay," she said when she walked in.

"You didn't see who stabbed me, did you?"

"Uh-no. I'd have said before now if I had. Don't *you* know?"

"No. I have ideas, but... no."

"There were some women in the store yesterday. They said they didn't know who stabbed you, but if they did they wouldn't tell. They think you deserved it."

"Golly, thanks for stopping by and telling me that. It's nice to know my neighbors hate me."

"You didn't already know that?"

She seemed genuinely surprised to discover I didn't know that. Of course, I don't always think a lot about my neighbors.

Opal was being annoying, so I changed the subject. "When are you going to go out with Cheryl Ann? I think she really likes you."

"Do you go out with people just because they like you?"

I didn't answer that. I did go out with a lot of guys just because they liked me, particularly if they liked me enough to buy me things.

"She's sweet," I said.

"I have a family history of diabetes."

"Oh my God, you're one of those girls, aren't you?"

"One of what girls?"

"The kind who only like people who treat them badly."

"I didn't come here to be insulted."

"Why did you come here?"

"I just came to be nice."

"Okay."

"Okay what?"

"Go ahead. Be nice."

She nearly growled at me, "Get well soon." And then she left.

Sometime later that afternoon, a middle-aged woman came in from billing and introduced herself, "I'm Leonora Scheck. I'm here to talk to you about your bill."

She didn't actually have to introduce herself, her name was on a tag pinned to the baby blue cardigan she wore.

"I have no insurance," I said. "I have no money. End of conversation," I said.

"Your grandmother is Emma Cole. She paid your last bill."

"I was stabbed. Someone tried to kill me. That's who you should be asking to pay my bill."

"That's not how this works."

"It should be."

"You can talk to a lawyer about suing whoever stabbed you. But in the meantime, we'll need to be paid."

"I barely make any money at all."

She sighed as though this was some kind of personal fault. "And why is that?"

"Why is what?"

"Why is it that you don't make any money? You're twenty-four years old, nearly twenty-five. You should have settled into some kind of career by now."

"I just got out of college," I said. Okay it was around two years ago but still.

"You have a college degree. Then you're eminently employable. You just need to get a decent job and we'll set up a payment plan. Your payments will probably be around a thousand a month. You'll want to get this paid off in the next five years."

"Oh my God, how much is the bill?

"At the moment, forty-five thousand dollars. Give or take."

"Okay, what do you do when people can't pay?"

"Can't or won't?"

"Can't."

Another heavy sigh. "Did you make under eight thousand nine hundred- and forty-one-dollars last year?"

"Kind of," I said.

"Did you, or didn't you?"

"No."

"Do you think you'll make under eight thousand nine hundred-and forty-one dollars this year?"

"Kind of," I said again.

I probably would make less than that if you didn't count the fifteen thousand dollar reward I'd gotten. Most of which had gone for taxes and a ridiculously large garnishment by a credit card company. The rest, which was much reduced, I'd spent on my car.

She stared at me until I admitted, "No."

"Well, that brings us back to your grandmother. Could you ask her to pay the bill?"

"Forty-five thousand dollars? No."

"But she's your family."

"Her maiden name is Scheck. Like yours. I'll bet we're cousins. Family. How much are you chipping in?"

"That isn't funny."

"It wasn't meant to be."

CHAPTER SEVENTEEN

Later that afternoon, Bev and Nana Cole came to collect me.

"Why didn't my mother come?"

"She's feeling fat today," my grandmother said.

"I don't see the problem. She was fat yesterday and she'll be fat tomorrow."

"She's not fat," Bev said. "She's pregnant."

That was splitting a hair. It's not that I wanted my mother to come with them, exactly. It's just that, occasionally she attempted to be a good mother. But I never really knew when she might give it a go and when it didn't even cross her mind. I'd almost prefer it if she was reliably awful at mothering.

I had to be taken to the exit of the hospital by an orderly, which meant a ride in a wheelchair. Really, I didn't feel that bad. I mean, I'd been given a Vicodin an hour before they released me. And... The surgeon said there weren't a lot of nerve endings when you got that deep inside, so all the messing around they did shouldn't bother me much. The muscles, though, they would be a problem. He gave me a prescription for three days of Vicodin. After that I was supposed to take Tylenol. Tylenol!

Anyway, Bev and the orderly helped me into the back seat

of her ancient Jeep Cherokee. When we were all in the car and ready to go, I said, "We need to go to the pharmacy, I need to fill a prescription."

That was met by silence. Eventually, as she pulled out of the hospital parking lot, Bev asked, "Which one."

"The one next to Benson's."

Nana Cole turned around in her seat, and said, "Give me the prescription."

That seemed like a terrible idea.

"That's all right," I said.

"You can stay in the car; I'll go in and get it for you."

"You limp. I can do it myself."

"You're in pain."

"I'm okay."

"If you're not in pain then we don't need to fill the prescription."

"I'm in pain."

"I'll do it," Bev said, mainly to stop our bickering, I think. "I'm completely mobile."

Reluctantly, I gave the prescription to Bev. My grandmother was up to something, I just didn't know what.

We were nearly all the way to Masons Bay when I realized that Ham had not come to see me at the hospital. I tried to count how many days it had been since I met him and figure out if he was even in town. Or had he run through his retainer and gone?

I turned around—ah, twisting was not a great idea—I tried to gently look over my shoulder. That didn't work either. I leaned so I could see through the side mirror on the passenger side and, yes, there was a black SUV behind us. Yup, that was Ham. Following us. I should probably not have felt so relieved, but I did. I was glad he hadn't gone. It was nice to have my own PI following me around. Not everyone was so lucky. Plus, I really wanted to find out who he thought might have stabbed me.

We pulled up in front of the drugstore and Ham pulled up next to us. Bev and Nana Cole got out of the Jeep and went inside the drugstore. As soon as they were inside, Ham got out and came over to the Jeep. I rolled my window down.

"How are you feeling?"

"Like I got stabbed."

"Do you have any idea who did it?"

"No. Do you?"

"Helena has decided you did it to yourself so you can sue her."

"Why does everyone have such a low opinion of me?"

Ignoring that, he went on, "I did find out something interesting. Robbie Jensen has been married twice and currently lives with a male Little League coach."

"You mean, she's straight?"

"Seems that way, yes. She's certainly a good friend of Helena's but apparently not a lover."

"Okay... I understand why Dr. Blinski's daughter-in-law might tell me something like that, given the family dynamic, but what about Cheryl Ann?"

He shrugged. "You're probably not the only person Sally Blinski told. She could be spreading that rumor around all over town."

"Do you think there's more to it than settling old grudges? Do you think Sally's trying to make it seem like Helena killed the doctor?"

"Could be. If there's no affair, there's no motive. In fact, I'd say Helena has the opposite of a motive. She needed the doctor to keep doing what he was doing. Without him, she'll eventually run out of money."

"Did you talk to her at the party?" he asked.

"Briefly. She made it sound like Nancy Fisher still thinks I did it, which was weird since she'd just apologized to me."

"Did anything else weird happen at book club?"

"Besides my being stabbed?"

"Yeah, besides that."

"Couple of things I'm thinking of following up. Hey, aren't you supposed to leave soon?"

"I got paid for another week."

"This can't be what Helena wants you to be doing, though. Talking to me about who stabbed me."

"I'm gaining your trust. I'm sure you'll confess soon," he said. I wasn't sure if he was joking.

He tipped an imaginary hat and got back into his Navigator. As he was driving off, Bev and Nana Cole came out of the drugstore. Once they were in the Jeep, I asked, "Can I have my medication?"

"I'm going to hold onto it," Nana Cole said.

"What? What are you talking about?"

"That nice doctor you had in the ER, he's the same one you had the last time you were there. He seemed to know a lot about you. He suggested I keep your medication and give it to you as directed. So that's what I'm going to do."

For a moment I got angry, really angry. That gorgeous bastard. What did he think he was doing? How dare he stick his perfect nose in where it didn't belong.

Then I remembered. I'd borrowed ten Oxy from Helena's medicine cabinet. I was pretty sure I'd put them into my pants pocket. Of course, now I was wearing a pair of jeans Nana Cole had brought for me.

"Hey, where are my clothes?"

"What clothes?"

"The ones I was wearing the night of book club."

"I'm sure they threw them away," Bev said. "They were covered in blood, you know."

It was my blood, so I did kind of know that. The whole thing was a tragedy. And not just because I lost ten Oxy, I really did love that shirt. Then I remembered I had a stash at home. So, yeah, Nana Cole could dole out the pills all she wanted. If I needed an extra half 10 here or there or even a whole 10, I'd just take it out of my stash. As we drove, Nana Cole and Bev started talking about Barbara.

"So you think she's doing better?" my grandmother asked.

"Oh, yes, much. She's still grieving, of course, but every day is a little better."

"She's barely talking to me."

"Can you blame her?"

"I'm her friend. I want to help."

"You can't Emma. You've always been so gung-ho about the war, but you never had anything at stake. She did and she lost."

"That doesn't mean I was wrong."

Bev didn't say anything. I wasn't sure how she felt about the war, we didn't talk about things like that. I thought it was wrong, but my grandmother would write me off as some hippy-dippy liberal who didn't know what he was talking about.

"She should get married again," Nana Cole said.

"What?" Bev said, turning to stare at her long enough that it made me uncomfortable. She was supposed to be driving.

"How long has it been since Walt died?"

"Fifteen years, I think."

"It's time. It would help with the grief if she had someone."

"I don't think taking care of some old man, feeding him, cleaning up after him, catering to him, is going to make up for losing her grandson."

"I didn't say it would. I said it would be a distraction."

"Why don't you get married again, Emma?"

"I don't think I'm cut out for that."

"And why do you think Barbara is?"

"I was trying to be nice."

"Nice would be apologizing to her for supporting a war that killed her grandson."

That comment resulted in a stony silence that lasted until we got home. I felt like Bev had gone too far, just like I'd gone too far when I'd blamed my grandmother for all violence against gay people. It wasn't that we were wrong so much… It was that one old lady in Michigan had very little power. I mean, yeah, she voted for terrible people, and she watched horrible TV shows, and she attempted to bully her friends into thinking the same horrible things. But the problem wasn't my grandmother, it was that there were millions like her. None of whom took responsibility for the pain their beliefs caused. So why did we think Nana Cole would be different?

When we got home, I painfully made my way out of the Jeep, into the house and up the stairs. I had to stop on the stairs and let things calm down for a moment. I knew Nana Cole wouldn't give me one of my pills for at least another two hours. All I had to do was get to my new bedroom and dip into my stash.

There had been some discussion in the car about sleeping arrangements. Nana Cole suggested I sleep on the sofa, which sounded like a nightmare. Not to mention, I did need to go upstairs to get my stash, so I'd insisted.

By the time I walked into the room, I was breathing in and out like a pregnant lady trying control her contractions. Like my mother will in a few weeks. Anyway, I went directly to the dresser where I'd hidden my main stash in a sock. Not a very original spot, but it had worked just fine for the last eight months. Until now. I opened the drawer and immediately saw that my stash and the sock I kept it in were gone.

Right away, I knew what had happened. I carefully walked down the hallway and opened my mother's door. She was lying on the twin bed with pillows under her knees and at her back. I couldn't even say where she'd gotten them all. She was reading a month-old *People Magazine* with Ben Affleck and Jennifer Lopez on the cover—*Will Their Love Survive!* It was my magazine. She'd taken it out of my room.

She looked up, and said, "One of the many, many shitty things about being pregnant is that now there is only one position I'm comfortable in. I can never quite remember it though."

"You stole my stash."

"I wouldn't call it stealing. I'd call it saving your life."

"I'm titrating down."

"Likely story."

"I'm also in a lot of pain."

"Ask your grandmother for a pill."

They were in this together. I spend two nights in the hospital, and they cook up a plot to torture me.

"You don't look good; you should go lie down," she said.

"I don't look good because I got stabbed."

"How did you manage that, by the way?"

"What? I didn't—"

"Obviously someone's really mad at you. I'm only getting little snippets. Your grandmother says you keep getting involved in these murders. Is that really a good idea?"

"You've made a lot of people really mad at you too."

"And yet I've never been stabbed."

This wasn't getting me what I wanted. "I don't understand, why are you suddenly so against drugs? You've always done drugs."

"Sure, marijuana, a little cocaine now and then, some ecstasy once in a awhile. I had a prescription for Valium for most of nineteen eighty-three. And eight-four. Yes, I've made a few bad decisions, but I never *overdosed*. And I've never been an *addict*."

These are the things she's proud of: That she's never been stabbed or overdosed. I was working up to saying something really mean, like I hoped her labor would last a month, but she changed the subject.

"I hear you got a big reward. You couldn't lend me a thousand, could you?"

CHAPTER EIGHTEEN

Twenty-four hours later, I was literally going insane. My new bedroom was directly above the kitchen, which meant I could hear most of went on down there through a poorly sealed furnace vent. Nana Cole and my mother fought most of that Saturday. Much of their arguing was about Johnny Cash. Apparently he'd died, and Nana Cole thought he was a god-fearing Christian man, while my mother argued he was a liberal icon. Neither considered the possibility he was both.

Late that afternoon, I called Ham and asked him to come and get me. When I reached the bottom of the stairs, having started down them nearly five minutes before, my grandmother was waiting, "Where do you think you're going?"

"Ham is picking me up."

That earned me a disdainful look.

"It's not like that. We're going to talk about who killed the doctor and who might have stabbed me."

Then my mother was there, looking over my grandmother's shoulder, saying, "I told him he needs to stop doing things like that."

She hadn't told me that exactly. "Are you talking about my getting accused of murder and getting stabbed?"

"Yes. It's not good."

"I know it's not good. You do realize I'm not the 'doing' part of either of those things. It's not like I woke up the other day and thought, 'Golly, it would be fun to get stabbed.'"

"Henry, take some responsibility." Said the woman who's never taken responsibility for anything in her life.

I stormed out of the house. Well, as much as a person can storm with thirty-six internal stitches and twenty-four external. Once I was outside and standing in the driveway, I waited for Ham. It was warm again. I guess it had been warm since book club, but I'd barely had time to notice. I'd been a little distracted.

The Navigator pulled up and I gingerly climbed in.

"Are you sure you should be doing this?"

"Absolutely. My family is driving me nuts."

"Yeah, I think that's the whole point of family."

"Ha-ha. Have you found anything out?"

"Not much. I've been questioning everyone who was at book club, trying to find someone who saw you stab yourself."

I rolled my eyes. "Seriously?"

"It also tells me who might have been close enough to stab you. So far, no one is admitting to being close enough to see what happened."

"That's crazy. The place was packed. There were people everywhere."

"I know. Right now, the best I've got is a list of people it's not. Your mother was talking to a guy named Joel Fletcher. He just bought the bookstore."

That was news. Phil Robins was the previous owner. He'd inherited quite a lot from Sammy Hart, my second, third or maybe fourth cousin who'd been murdered. I wondered if he'd left town completely or had just decided to stop working? Anyway...

"So it's not Joel Fletcher."

"Right."

"And it wasn't Reverend Wilkie because he was talking to my grandmother."

"Also right. And it's not Helena or Robbie Jensen, they were at the far end of the room. Several people saw Helena rush over after you were stabbed."

"What about Nancy Fisher?"

"She was in the foyer, with her daughter and her nephew putting their coats on. They were leaving."

"Are you sure about that? Because her nephew, Elbert, threatened me just a few minutes before I was stabbed."

"I'll double check, see if anyone saw him in the foyer other than Nancy and her daughter. Why do you think he threatened you?"

"The day I picked up my phone and laptop from the sheriff, I drove by the doctor's office. There was a truck with boxes in front. I thought Nancy might have been packing up the files, but when I asked her about it she said she wasn't."

"I saw that truck too. Her nephew thought that was you threatening her?"

"I guess."

"Then she was probably lying. Which means she could have been lying about where she was when you were stabbed."

"What about Sue Langtree?" I asked. "Did you figure out where she was standing?"

He gave me a funny look. "She's an old lady. I don't think she stabbed you."

I did not want to get into why that didn't matter and why she might have stabbed me.

After a questioning silence, he continued. "She said she was on the other side of the room. But that's what everyone said. No one else mentioned where she was. You think she has a reason to stab you?"

"Well, kind of. I don't want to talk about it though." To distract him, I said, "We should go talk to Sally Blinski again. Ask her why she lied about Helena and Robbie Jensen."

"Not a bad idea."

We drove out to M22 and turned toward Bellflower. It took a bit less than twenty-five minutes to arrive at Second Street. I'd spent most of the trip complaining about my grandmother and my mother. Ham listened and occasionally said useless things like, "You could try looking at it from their perspective" and "Pregnant women can be prone to some severe mood swings."

I was still ten feet behind when Ham rang the Blinski's doorbell. A guy around my mother's age opened the door. Jacob Blinski. It had to be him, given that he was opening the door and he looked like his younger brother Peter. Carefully, I climbed the porch steps.

Ham introduced us. Kind of. "I'm Hamlet Gilbody, private detective, and this is Henry Milch. We'd like to talk to you about your father's death." Which made it sound like we were working together, or he was working for me. Actually, he made it sound like anything but what it was.

Before Jacob could say anything, Sally came to the front of the house asking, "Honey, who is it?" When she saw us, she said, "Oh. You came back."

"They were here before?" Jacob asked his wife.

"Yeah. Well, that one was here before," she said, pointing at me.

"You told me that your mother-in-law was having an affair with her Pilates instructor," I said. "But we don't think that's true."

Jacob looked at her, and said, "Sally?"

"I saw something once. I mean, there might have been something going on. And I might have exaggerated a little."

"Maybe you should come inside," Jacob said, stepping out of the way so we could enter.

In the living room, I carefully lowered myself onto the flower-printed sofa. Once we were settled, Ham asked Sally,

"Why did you tell Henry that story about your mother-in-law and her Pilates instructor?"

"Because I love my husband and Helena hurt his family."

"Sally," Jacob said with disappointment in his voice. "You shouldn't have done that."

"When was the last time you saw your father?" I asked. I wasn't sure why I asked, but I had a feeling...

"A few weeks ago."

Now it was his wife's turn, "Jacob..."

"We've been meeting on the Turtlehead trail." As he spoke, I noticed that he would look at Ham but not at me. That was obnoxious.

"We'd hike together for a half mile or so. I didn't tell anyone because, well, I wasn't sure I could defend it. He wasn't sorry, exactly, but he did seem to regret the things that happened. He called divorcing my mother unfortunate. Which is not exactly taking responsibility."

"Do you have any idea who might have killed him?" Ham asked.

"I don't. I'm sorry."

"What was your father's state of mind?" I asked. Super broad question, probably too broad.

"I know that things with Helena weren't good," he said, still not looking at me. "He was thinking about retiring. She wasn't happy about that. I know he was concerned that he wasn't really helping his patients."

Almost immediately, I realized that if he was truly thinking about retiring then Helena had a motive again.

"Jacob, why didn't you tell me? I'd have liked to have met him. He was your father, after all."

"I was trying to decide if he was a good person or not. Obviously, he did bad things. Sometimes good people do. Honestly, I'm still not sure about him. I might never be."

"I could have helped you decide," she said, softly.

"I talked to your brother, Peter. He said that Helena was

almost a member of your family when she was your father's nurse. Can you tell us about that?"

To Ham, he said, "She and Wayne spent holidays with us for years. He was just a kid, much younger than we were. We were all in our twenties and thirties. My mother would do her best to get us all together. She and Helena would put out a feast. They were friends. I remembered they'd go down to Grand Rapids shopping together."

"How long do you think the affair was going on?" I asked.

Sally reached out and rested her hand on her husband's. He turned gave her a smile before he started. Now, he kept looking at her. "Looking back, a long time. There were things that didn't make sense until later. About six months after Helena started working for my father, she bought a new car. A little BMW. She always had nicer clothes than my mother. Always wore jewelry. Before we asked, she'd talk about a settlement she got from Wayne's father or an inheritance from an aunt. But around that time my parents began having money problems. My sister Susannah wanted to go to graduate school and he told her they couldn't afford to help. And Peter, well, he'd been messing around since high school. He got it together for a while and wanted help going to college. My father said he couldn't, didn't have the money."

I turned to Sally, "You said you never met your father-in-law? The divorce was only seven years ago."

"We married late."

Jacob gave a fuller explanation. "I was married in my twenties. We divorced. Not like my parents, though. It's been friendly. We have a daughter who just graduated high school."

I glanced at Sally to see if he might be lying about how friendly things were, but her expression was placid. It did explain why he'd been trying to cut his father some slack, though.

"You know, Helena's only six years older than my sister

Lena. I think that's a lot of why we didn't see what was happening."

I looked at Ham to see if he had any more questions. He seemed not to, so I stood up. As we began to walk out of their living room, I heard Sally say, "Oh no."

Turning around, I saw a round circle of blood on her sofa. Apparently, I'd been leaking. I tried on an apologetic look; not sure if it worked.

"Salt," I said. "I've heard that will get it out."

FORTUNATELY, they were very gracious about my having bled all over their furniture. Before we left, Ham asked for a garbage bag to put over the seat of his SUV. It was all vaguely humiliating. I was now this person who couldn't control his bodily fluids. This person who'd show up at your house and leave part of himself on your sofa.

After he spread the garbage bag over the seat and I climbed in, Ham said, "We're done for today. You shouldn't have come out."

"I couldn't stay there any longer."

"Do you need to go to the emergency room?"

"I'm sure it's fine."

"Lean forward, I need to take a look." I did as I was told. He lifted up my shirt. Fortunately, I was wearing a B-52's t-shirt that I kind of hated. For one thing, it was two sizes too big; for another, my mother bought it for me when she dragged me to a B-52's concert for my twenty-first birthday. Her idea of a gift was to drag me to see one of her favorite bands. Clueless.

"You definitely need to change this bandage."

I probably should have done that before I left the house.

"But I don't see any ripped stitches. It wouldn't be a bad idea to go to the emergency room though."

"Nope. Not happening. No way."

Seriously, I couldn't afford it.

Ham shut the passenger door and walked around to the driver's side. When we were moving, I asked, "Did you notice that guy wouldn't look at me?"

"Yeah. I did."

"What do you think was going on?"

He left an uncomfortable pause before he said, "I think you know."

And I did. "Do I have a neon sign on my head that says 'faggot'?"

"You are literally wearing a yellow neon shirt."

And here we had a disagreement. I would call it mustard, which is not the same as neon yellow at all. But that didn't change his point.

Ham asked, "Do you think we learned anything important from them?"

"Helena's back on the list as a suspect. If the doctor was going to retire, he might have reached the point where he was worth more dead than alive."

He was quiet, then said, "What about Nancy Fisher? She's younger than Helena. Do you think it's possible the doctor had a thing going on with her?"

That was an interesting idea. Nancy was in her forties, but her gray hair made her look older. I mean, I hadn't considered it. Why would I? I knew absolutely nothing about what old straight men found attractive.

"Is Helena that stupid?" I asked. "I mean, wouldn't she make sure the doctor didn't do to her what he did to his first wife?"

"What about the local drug dealer? The one in the trailer park."

"You think he killed the doctor to get rid of the competition?"

"Makes sense, doesn't it?"

"He mostly sells weed."

"Maybe he thought it was time to expand his business."

I felt like he was trying to lead me away from Helena. Did he not believe she had something to do with it? Or did he just want to keep taking her money? Or was he actually trying to do what she wanted and find a way to pin it on me?

We talked about other possibilities. The Blinski children; there were two we hadn't spoken to. One didn't even live nearby, but that didn't mean he couldn't have come in, killed his father, and left. And there was the doctor's ex-wife. She also didn't live here. She could have—but she seemed to have moved on. Why would she kill him now?

CHAPTER NINETEEN

And then I slept for most of the next eighteen hours. My mother brought me my medicine, I'd wake up and take it, then I'd go back to sleep. I think I sleepwalked downstairs to the bathroom a couple of times. And at some point, I put a pillow over the vent, so I didn't have to listen to my mother and Nana Cole attempting to get along.

When I finally came to it was around ten on Sunday morning. I popped down to the bathroom first and took a much-needed shower, changing my bandage in the process. I had, fortunately, stopped bleeding. I pulled my SpongeBob pajama bottoms back on and an over-sized gray sweatshirt that said UCLA. The color of the shirt matched the cloudy sky outside the window.

Then I went into the kitchen to have breakfast. My mother was sitting at the table with nothing in front of her. She seemed odd. I made a pot of coffee in the Mr. Coffee and put a couple pieces of bread into the toaster. Finally, I'd had enough.

"Why are you just sitting there?"

"This is the only comfortable chair I could find."

It was straight-backed and wooden. It didn't even have a cushion.

"Don't look at me like that. I know it's not a 'comfortable' chair. It just is right now. Okay?"

"You want some coffee?"

She just glared at me. "Oh, that's right. Pregnant women can't have coffee." We'd done this already.

"If I had coffee right now this kid would rip its way out."

I decided not to mention that was pretty much what would be happening to her very soon. "How about some toast?"

"I'll just have some of yours. Can you make it with sugar and cinnamon?"

When the toast popped up, I put two more pieces of bread into the toaster, then buttered, sugared and cinnamoned the first two. With my coffee I sat down at the table.

Reaching out, she ripped off a chunk of toast—as though she wasn't going to eat the whole piece—and asked me, "So, are you going to start being nice to me?"

"Are you going to explain why you're broke? Or what you're doing here? Or what your plans are?"

"I guess I'll take that as a no."

Of course, I knew that her boyfriend was up to something, and since her name was on his companies, she was too. It was on the tip of my tongue to ask if the FBI was going to show up and break down the door. Instead, I asked, "Where's Nana Cole?"

"Church. One of her friends came and got her."

"Are you in trouble for not going?"

"When I was a girl, I used to hide in the bottom of my closet when it was time for church hoping they wouldn't find me."

That didn't answer my question exactly but, hey, whatever. Then I asked, "You went to school with Jacob Blinski, didn't you?"

"A long time ago."

"Yeah, but you remember him, don't you?"

She shrugged and ate some more toast. "He was always a

Goody Two-shoes. He tried to start some kind of Kids for Christ group. I didn't have much to do with him. I was more of a stoner."

That seemed weird, so I asked, "Random question. How did you end up Cherry Queen if you were a stoner?"

"I was a pretty *hot* stoner. And look out the window. We own a cherry orchard. That worked in my favor."

"Nana Cole is proud of that. You being a Cherry Queen."

"One of the few things I ever did right."

"What about Nancy Fisher? Did you go to school with her?"

"She was a couple years ahead of me."

"You remember anything about her?"

"Why do you care? The sheriff's not going to arrest you. You're in the clear."

"Technically, I'm still not supposed to leave town. And I'd like to."

"You do know that 'don't leave town' routine only works on TV. You can go anywhere you want to."

That was probably true. But, well, he was a sheriff, so I believed him. Besides, I didn't have the money to leave town yet. Well, I didn't have the money to get an apartment. I could leave town. It's just that being homeless in Los Angeles wasn't my favorite thing.

"Nancy Fisher was Nancy Hagen in school. She had four or five sisters, I think. Two of them were at book club."

"Really?"

"Yeah. Debbie, I don't think she's a Hagen anymore, but I don't remember who she married. And Leeann, I don't know much about her."

"Nancy's nephew is named Elbert. Was his mother there? Is she Debbie or Leeann?"

She shrugged. "Your grandmother might know. Debbie was best friends with Helena in high school. I remember that." She ate the last of the piece of toast she hadn't wanted.

I got up and made some more.

Then she asked, "Are you happy about having a sibling?"

"Sure, I've been wanting someone to play blocks with."

She just stared at me.

"I'd be happier if you were just a bit more stable. Dragging me through two husbands and six boyfriends probably wasn't the best thing for me."

"I wouldn't say that. You got good grades. You put yourself through college. You lived on your own for years. You've been taking care of your grandmother. I'd say I made you self-reliant."

"By neglecting me."

"I gave you room to grow. You should be thanking me."

Well, I wasn't about to do that.

"So, don't you need a lot of stuff when you have a baby? Like, car seats and diapers and bottles and crap like that?"

"There's stuff in the boxes you put on the porch. Didn't you look? Your grandmother never throws out anything."

I wasn't sure my mother's baby things would do her much good. Things had changed in the last forty-odd years. Probably a lot. But I decided not to ask any more questions about that. It wasn't my problem after all.

The backdoor opened and, leading with her cane, my grandmother stomped her way inside. Behind her were Bev and Barbara. As soon as the women were all in the kitchen, I could see that Nana Cole and Barbara were both red-eyed. I wondered if my grandmother had actually apologized the way Bev had told her to. She must have. They were all together and they seemed comfortable. And there had clearly been tears.

"You made coffee, Emily, that's wonderful," Bev said.

Before I could say *I* made the coffee, Barbara asked, "Are you excited? I'll bet you can't wait to meet your baby. Emma says you don't know what you're having. I think that's best. Let it be a surprise."

Nana Cole sat down between us. "Do you need a pillow, dear? I'll have Henry get you one."

"I need a rolled-up towel."

"Henry."

My mouth fell open, but still, I picked my way down the hallway to the bathroom. Why weren't people waiting on me? I got stabbed, isn't that worse than being pregnant? I was violently attacked; she got laid. Seriously, she should be the one running down the hall for a towel. Not that I needed one, but you know what I mean.

I brought the towel back and offered it to my mother.

"Could you just slip it back there? Where the curve in my back used to be."

I did what she asked.

"The last few weeks are the hardest," Barbara said.

"I don't know," Nana Cole said. "Morning sickness can be hard to get through."

"I was stabbed like three days ago," I blurted out.

"Yes, dear, we know," my grandmother said. "Why don't you go find your dog. I'm sure he's up to no good."

As I angrily left the room, my mother raised an eyebrow as though to say, "Ha-ha."

OUTSIDE, I picked up a tennis ball and threw it for Riley. Like, I said, it never worked with him. But then, he bolted after it. At first, I was surprisingly happy. And then I realized my throwing a ball was probably not a good idea. If I kept it up, I'd pop a stitch.

Ham's Navigator sat at the end of our driveway. I confused poor Riley, who'd gotten the ball and brought it back to me to throw again, by turning and walking walked down the driveway.

Seeing me coming, Ham got out of the Navigator and

leaned up against it. He didn't look like a private eye. No trench coat. No fedora. No cloud of cigarette smoke nearby. He looked like a young dad: Cubs baseball hat, Polo shirt, loose jeans, and Reeboks. Like a lot of straight guys, he managed to be in style and out of style at the same time.

"How you feeling?" he asked when I got close.

"Like someone stabbed me three days ago. Anything going on?"

"I've been looking closely at Ronnie Sheck. He seems to be operating pretty openly. Why do you think he's getting away with it?"

I'd never really thought about that, but now that he said it, it seemed pretty true. There were a number of possibilities. First, Sheriff Crocker could be totally corrupt. Definitely a possibility. Second, maybe Ronnie was too small to worry about. Sandy with the yurt said she grew pot for him. Maybe he had other local growers. Which would mean he wasn't closely connected to organized crime. So why go after him? If they took him down that would leave a vacuum for someone worse to fill. Someone potentially violent.

"I don't really know," I said. "Could be a lot of things."

"What do you know about the guys who are always hanging around?"

"Did you go in there and buy something?"

"Of course. I had to check it out."

"What have you got?"

"None of your business."

"Oh, come on."

"I'm not giving you drugs. Not right now. You've got painkillers from your surgery."

"My grandmother's doling them out."

"And we're not going to mess with that."

"Yeah, yeah, yeah. If I die Helena's gonna want a refund."

"Exactly. And also... you amuse me."

Was that a compliment? It really didn't sound like one.

Fools were amusing. Buffoons were amusing. This was not something I'd ever aspired to.

Helena's son had gone to prison for having several pounds of marijuana. Ronnie was probably smart enough to never have too much around. That might explain the guys who were always hanging around. He probably split his merchandise between them, so no one ever had enough... And then it hit me. Elbert was one of those guys. That's why I thought he looked familiar at book club.

"Elbert," I said. "Elbert—Nancy Fisher's nephew. He's one of the guys who hangs out with Ronnie."

"So, he could have given the doctor's schedule to Ronnie."

That was one way to look at it.

CHAPTER TWENTY

My mother went into labor in the middle of the night. She knocked on my door at like three o'clock in the morning.

"Henry, it started. I want to go to the hospital."

"When? When did it start?"

"Maybe an hour."

"Okay, well, doesn't this take a long time? Can I get like a couple more hours of sleep?"

She opened the door, and said, "No, we need to go now."

I groaned and sat up in bed. Riley was lying on his side. He looked like he was trying to ignore this. I couldn't blame him.

"Hurry up."

"Can I change my clothes?"

"No. You're covered head to toe." She was right. I'd been sleeping in my SpongeBob pajama bottoms and a big T-shirt. Yes, you're right, I tend to wear more clothes to bed than I do in public. Big deal.

My mother said, "Let's go."

God, she was annoying.

"What's going on? Is it time?" Nana Cole called up the stairs.

"I don't want to do this!" my mother called down the stairs. "This is a terrible idea."

"Yes, of course, dear. Did you pack a bag like I told you?"

"Kind of. Oh my God—" She stopped midway down the stairs, holding onto the railing so tightly I thought she might break it off.

"Henry, go grab your mother's bag."

"I'm not supposed to pick things up."

"Oh, it can't be that heavy." Then to my mother she said, "Take deep breaths, dear."

"That doesn't work. They just act like it does so they can sell videotapes. I need drugs."

"When you get to the hospital."

My mother turned around, rushed up two steps, and grabbed me by the arm. "You have another stash, don't you? Give me a little something to get me to the hospital."

I didn't have another stash. And if I did have another stash, I wouldn't share it with her. Not after she stole my first stash, which apparently she'd unwisely flushed down the toilet.

"I'm going to grab your bag."

In her bedroom, her suitcase sat on the floor partly full. I had no idea what else she might need, so I just closed it and picked it up. It was heavy. I tried to imagine why she might need to bring bricks to the hospital. I switched it to the hand opposite my wound and went downstairs hoping I wasn't shredding myself.

My mother and grandmother were heading out the front door.

Slowly, we moved toward the cars. My grandmother had turned on every light inside and out. It felt like a movie set. Losing patience, I got in front of them and headed toward the Escalade. But the wound in my back gave me a few jabs reminding me to slow down.

Behind me my mother said, "Oh no, no way, I'm not

climbing up into that thing. I learned my lesson after book club. We're taking yours Henry."

"How's Nana Cole going to get into the backseat?"

"I'll manage. I'm better at crawling than walking."

I wasn't sure I wanted to know how she knew that. We reached my car, and I opened the passenger's side. After I flipped the seat forward, Nana Cole shoved her cane at me then scrambled ungracefully into the back seat. I handed her the cane, then asked for the blanket I'd thrown back there in case I needed to take Riley anywhere. I placed it over the passenger seat.

"What's that for?" she asked. "You think I'm going to leak?"

"You are going to leak. You've done this before, right?"

"Don't be so disrespectful to you mother, Henry," Nana Cole said from the back.

My mother stuck her tongue out at me. I stepped back to wait while she got into the car.

"Aren't you going to help me?" she snarled. I really didn't know how she wanted to be helped. She put one hand on the top of the door and the other on the seat and began lowering herself. I put a hand on her head so that she wouldn't hit the convertible top just the way the police put a suspect into a squad car. It was pretty likely she'd been committing some kind of white-collar crime, so it was appropriate.

She couldn't get the seat belt around her. I had to help her try to extend it, but once we'd done that it still didn't reach all the way. We gave up. I walked slowly around the car and got in. As I was turning the ignition, my mother said, "Can't you move any faster?" The beeper for her seatbelt began going off.

"You'll recall, I recently had surgery," I said. And, yes, I was very snippy when I said it.

"You'll recall, I'm having a baby *now*—ah, oh, ouch, ouch, ouch, ouch."

"You're having a contraction?" Nana Cole asked from the backseat.

"Of course I'm having a contraction."

"That's seven minutes since the last one. We have plenty of time. Stay within the speed limit, Henry."

"I'm your mother. Break every traffic law in the book."

It was a moot point. My car wasn't capable of breaking traffic laws. The beeper for the seatbelt was still going off. Super annoying.

"How long does it take for that thing to stop?" Nana Cole asked.

"I don't know. I've never driven with anyone who couldn't wear a seat belt."

I thought it was kind of me not to say my mother was too fat to wear a seat belt.

"I think the only way to stop it is to click it together. Maybe you could lean forward and click it behind your back."

"Really? You think I'm that limber."

"Lean forward," Nana Cole said in her most no-nonsense voice.

She undid her own safety belt and pushed herself up against the back of the seat and reached her arms around. I was only getting glimpses of this, since I was already at the end of the driveway and about to turn south toward Bellflower. I heard a click and the beeping stopped.

"Thank you, Mother."

I pulled out onto M22 and floored my way through the gears. We weren't going very fast, which prompted my mother to ask, "Is this as fast as it goes?

It seemed an appropriate time to ask, "What did you do with my Honda?"

"Your Honda? That was my car that I let you use."

"You gave it to me. For my high school graduation. You put a bow on it."

"It was always in my name."

"For insurance purposes. That's what you told me."

"I don't remember saying that. Besides, the use of a car for six years is still a gift."

"You sold it didn't you?"

"Of course, I sold it. It was *my* car."

The annoying thing about this conversation was that my mother never bought her own car. They were bought or leased by different boyfriends. Frank bought her the Honda and then foolishly put it in her name.

"What did you do with the money?"

"I spent it. That's what you do with money."

"It was my money. Kind of."

Then she had a conveniently placed contraction. "Ah, fuck, fuck, fuck..."

"Just breathe, dear."

"Shut up."

When it was over, I could feel her staring at me.

"How dare you?"

I wasn't quite sure what she meant by that. *Had I missed something?* I said, "Me? Why me? I didn't have anything to do with your current situation."

"I gave birth to you. I fed you. I bought you everything you ever needed, and I did it *all by myself!*"

Nana Cole cleared her throat in the back.

"I did it mostly by myself."

Nana Cole cleared her throat again.

"I did a lot of it. A whole lot of it."

"Yeah, but I didn't ask you to have me, did I? A contract made by one person isn't enforceable."

"A contract? You think motherhood is a contract? So, you're a lawyer now?"

"You don't have to be a lawyer to understand that it takes more than one living, existing person to make a contract. You can only hold me responsible for things I agreed to. Which, by the way, was not very much."

"Oh Henry, get over yourself. You're too old to be this angry at me."

"And you're not still angry at your mother?"

"That's different."

"Hold on," Nana Cole said. "Emily, most of the bad things that have happened in your life are things I told you not to do. You can't blame *everything* on me."

"Oh fine. Gang up on the pregnant lady."

She had another contraction, which I was sure she was faking. It was much too soon. We managed to get through the rest of the drive without ripping each other apart which meant we remained mostly silent.

When we arrived at Midland Hospital (formerly Morley Medical Center, formerly St. Anne's) I pulled up to the emergency entrance, got out, gingerly walked around the car and yanked my mother out of the passenger seat. Then I pulled my grandmother out of the back.

While they made their way inside, I parked the car. By the time I got into the ER waiting room, they'd already been taken in. I stopped at the triage nurse and told her I'd just dropped my mother off and asked if I could go back.

"Does she want you there?"

Well, that was a tricky question, right up there with 'Did I want to be there?' There was actually a lot about to happen that I would not want to be there for. We were still in a safe zone though, so I said, "Oh, of course she does."

The nurse nodded, then ignored me. I walked through double doors. Unfortunately, I know my way around Midland's ER. It wasn't a busy night, so only one bay was curtained off. I went right to it, slid the curtain to one side, and went in.

Immediately, my mother said "Henry!"

That's when I realized Dr. Edward Stewart had his head between her legs. Didn't this man ever take a day off? I looked up at the ceiling red-faced. Trust me, the only thing between my mother's legs I wanted to gawk at was Edward.

I squeezed my way down to my mother's chest, squashing my Nana Cole in the process.

"Henry, don't step on me."

"Sorry."

Edward's head popped up. Rather than hello, he said, "I'm not sure you should be out of bed yet. There wasn't anyone else who could have brought your mother in?"

"She insisted."

"It's the middle of the night. I don't fit behind the wheel, my mother can't drive after her stroke, Henry has been— Is this really the most important thing right now?"

"Everything looks fine, Mrs.—"

"Emily. You just looked up my hoo-ha. You can use my first name."

"Emily, you're dilating nicely. We'll move you up to the maternity ward in just a few minutes. This should all be wrapped up sometime in the next ten hours or so."

"Ten hours? Ten *fucking* hours? I need drugs."

I was right. I could have slept longer.

"Your OB/GYN should have prepared you for this. I don't mean to be rude but—how old are you?"

Before she could answer, I said, "Forty-three."

"I wasn't going to lie."

She was totally going to lie.

"Yes, well, yours is a geriatric pregnancy. Older mothers often have low birth weight babies or higher birth weight babies. It looks like you're on the higher end of the scale. That could present some challenges. Again, your OB/GYN should have warned you about that. Are you seeing someone locally?"

I was so tempted to tell him she hadn't seen anyone anywhere, but she sidestepped the issue by saying, "I'm visiting from California."

The smile on his face suggested he knew what she wasn't saying. Good for him.

"I'll just go call maternity," he said, then looked at me and tipped his head a tiny bit.

As soon as he left, I said, "Excuse me. Bathroom." And walked out of the bay. Edward was standing at a nurses' station on the far side of the ER. I walked over and presented myself.

He looked me up and down saying, "Nice PJs."

"Thanks. I wanted the *Macbeth* ones, but they were all out."

"So, after you were stabbed, I heard something weird. People think you killed Dr. Blinski."

My God, did rumors never die in this town?

"What do you think?"

"I'd say you didn't kill him."

"Well, there you go."

"The thing about the doctor being killed though, it got me thinking."

"Afraid you'll be next?"

"No. Not at all. The night we sort of had a date..."

"I don't want to talk about that."

"Well, I wasn't trying to. I'm trying to talk about that *day*. That day, you might remember, I had a patient overdose."

Nope, did not remember that.

"She was a girl named Ally. I'm pretty sure she was Dr. Blinski's patient. I think a lot of the overdoses we get are his patients."

"Ally?" That clicked right away. "Was she here alone?"

"Her brother brought her in. She wasn't breathing. He couldn't tell me what she'd taken. She had been drinking, which made it worse. It all happened very quickly."

Guilt was etched into his pretty face. Somehow it just made him prettier.

"We've been getting a lot of overdoses. Too many. Several

a month. We save most of them. Of course, some of them die at home and we never see them."

"Ally's family says she died of a bee sting. Is that possible?"

"No, it's not," he said sternly. "I know the difference between anaphylactic shock and a drug overdose."

"Sorry. I don't. That's why I asked. So, weird question. You put overdose on her death certificate?"

"I don't make out the death certificate. I just provide time of death to the funeral home. They have the attending physician sign the certificate."

"Dr. Blinski?"

"Yes."

"You think he put bee sting to cover it up? How do I get a copy?"

"County clerk's office. But if I call Heartwell's they might tell me. That would be faster."

"Would you do that?"

"Yeah. I'm curious myself."

The conversation seemed over, so I said, "Thanks. And thanks for taking care of my mother."

"She hasn't had much prenatal care, has she?"

"No. None that I know of."

"I'll let them know upstairs. It will help." Then he asked, "How are things going for you? With the pills, I mean. I'd hate for something to happen to you."

"Things are peachy. I'm titrating down. My little problem will be solved in just a couple of days. You don't have to worry."

"You're not having a lot of withdrawal symptoms?"

"A little bit of nausea, headache, hot flashes, the occasional bout of the shivers."

He took a prescription pad and a pen out of his coat's side pocket. Quickly, he wrote out a prescription. Held it out to me.

"What is that?"

I didn't take it. I'd heard about drugs that make you so sick you didn't want Oxy anymore. That was a game I didn't feel like playing.

"It's Ativan. It's enough for five days. On your last day of OxyContin start taking it. It should take the edge off the symptoms. Just don't get any ideas about continuing Ativan. It's also addictive."

Well, there goes that plan.

I took the prescription. Ativan was just like Valium. And I could always get more Valium from Bev. And, on the bright side, I couldn't get enough from her to get addicted so it wouldn't matter if I pinched a couple every now and then. Maybe my near future wasn't as dreary as I thought.

I left my mother and grandmother at the hospital without saying goodbye. I knew they didn't need me, but they wouldn't necessarily agree. Best to slink off.

CHAPTER TWENTY-ONE

Ten hours. That meant I didn't have to go back to the hospital until two o'clock. I went home, found where my grandmother kept my Vicodin, took one, and then hid the bottle on the top shelf in the closet. She'd have to get on a chair to reach it, and at the moment, she couldn't do that. Then I went to sleep.

About four hours later, my phone started ringing. I knew it was probably my grandmother asking where I was—and probably telling me not to touch my Vicodin—so I didn't answer. Then, my phone made the doorbell tone. I'd assigned that to texts. Not that I got many, I was *not* a teenager. Still, I was curious. My grandmother certainly would not have sent me a text.

I picked up my flip phone and saw that the text message was from Ham. MEET @ NF HOUSE ASAP. Okay, that was interesting. That was pretty much what I'd been planning to do next. Once I woke up or my mother had the baby or—well, next chance I got.

ASAP meant I skipped a shower and got dressed. That was a dilemma. What to wear to talk to someone you think is a murderer. Very different than dressing for a night of clubbing, right? But my wardrobe leaned heavily on evening wear. I decided on my grandfather's brown bowling shirt—which had his name, SAM, in a red circle—and pair of jeans.

When I got out to my car, I dialed 411, asked for Nancy Fisher, and when the operator said, "Hold for the number," I said, "Actually, can I get her address?"

She gave it to me. Repeating it to myself, I put my little phone onto the console in front of the shifter-thingie and took a gas station map out of the glove compartment.

She lived on M22 just north of Masons Bay. The map told me she must live near Jacktown Beach, which was part of Little Bear National Park. It was easy to get to, but I was still glad I looked at my map.

It took nearly forty minutes to get there, but all that meant was that Ham and I could spend hours questioning Nancy Fisher and I'd still get back in time for my mother's giving birth. Not that I really needed to be there. I was *not* going to be in the delivery room. That was an idea that horrified both me and my mother.

I was nearly there when my phone rang. Ham again. Calling this time. I grabbed the phone off the console and clicked on.

"Five minutes, relax."

"Hurry," Ham said, then immediately clicked off.

Weird, totally weird, I thought. Setting my phone back onto the console, I pulled into Nancy's driveway, which was quite large. Ham's Navigator was there, of course. The house was old and large. It was on the water so it had to be worth a lot of money, but just standing in front of it, I could tell it needed work. Nancy must have inherited the house. Clearly, she couldn't afford it on her nurse's salary.

It was one story and sprawling, probably built in the late fifties, maybe sixties. There was a two-car garage. I walked up to the front door and rang the bell. Waited. Nothing.

I squeezed in behind a boxy bush and looked through a window. The living room was nicely decorated without too much furniture. I could see the lake out the sliding doors on the far side of the room.

I walked around the house to the sprawling back lawn. There was a kind of gazebo near the water with a table and chairs. Nancy probably ate there with her husband. Wait. Did she have a husband? I wasn't even sure. I mean, there was a Mr. Fisher at some point. Was he around? Did they divorce? Was he dead? No idea.

Then I saw her standing at the end of a long metal dock. I guess I could have asked her, 'Hey Nancy, are you currently married?' and 'Did you kill Dr. Blinski?' Very important questions. Well, one of them was. I walked down to the dock. She had her back to me, looking out at the lake. Lake Michigan is more like an ocean than a lake. Logically, I know that the Pacific is much larger. Realistically, they're both bodies of water from which I can't see the other side.

When I got close, Nancy turned around, hugging a thick, brown cardigan tight against her.

"I've been expecting you."

I was trying to come up with a clever retort, when she allowed her cardigan to fall open, and pointed the gun she was holding right at me. She wore a pair of bright blue latex gloves that definitely did not go with that sweater.

"Okay, I guess you *were* expecting me."

She could have just shot me. People do, don't they? But she seemed nervous, anxious, fidgeting—murder is much easier in theory. In practice in can be—well, messy. And a bit emotional.

"He deserved to die; you know," she said. "He caused so much pain. Now the pain will stop. People will stop losing their children. Their parents. Their loved ones. The world is a better place without him. Don't you see that?"

"Did you know Dr. Blinski was writing Oxy prescriptions for your niece, Ally?"

"No, I didn't. I mean, I knew Ally was seeing him a lot. She was always prone to UTIs."

"What is that?"

"Urinary tract infection. She'd had them since she was a teenager. I didn't think much of it. It just seemed like they were getting worse, that's all. I told her she should see a specialist."

"You knew all along she didn't die of a bee sting? Did you confront the doctor about that?"

"I did. He said he'd done us a favor putting that on the death certificate. No one would know she was a drug addict."

"And that's when you decided to kill him?"

"No. I mean, I didn't decide. I—I wasn't serious. At my daughter's wedding, I had a bit too much to drink. I told Elbert how I'd go about killing the doctor if I had the nerve. I also told him I didn't have the nerve. I wasn't serious. It was weeks before the doctor's death. I thought it was something we joked about and then... well, you know what happened."

"It was your nephew, Elbert who climbed through the window wasn't it? You told him a good time to do it. You told him where the scalpel would be."

"Yes, but I wasn't serious, I just told you."

"When did you get serious?"

"I knew right away Elbert had done it. And there you were, covered in blood. I had to make it seem like you'd done it. It was the right thing to do."

I could hear resolve in her voice. We were going in the wrong direction; resolve might get me killed.

"Helena knew what happened?" I asked.

She nodded. "She's Elbert's godmother. I knew she'd protect him."

"That's why she hired a PI to prove I did it," I said.

"It would have been the best thing for us if you went to prison."

"It didn't matter to you that I was innocent?"

"You're not innocent. You're a drug addict and a little fairy. Why would anyone care what happened to you?"

Wow, that was unexpected. I guess I shouldn't have been surprised. She'd basically talked her nephew into killing a person. Why would she care who paid the price for his crime? As long as it wasn't Elbert it didn't matter.

"How are you planning to explain my dead body?"

"I doubt I'll have to. Your body will end up in the lake, the current will take it away. Did you see the weather report today? High probability of rip currents. If I put a few stones in your pockets, it's unlikely your body will ever be found."

"What if it is?"

"I won't be the first person they question."

Okay, now she was sounding a lot more serious about this. The possibility that she might *actually* shoot me was getting likelier and likelier. Which meant I probably needed to do something. Anything. It wasn't such a great idea to stand there waiting to be shot.

I decided I should probably rush her. I decided to bend over and try to tackle her. Yes, it was entirely possible she'd shoot me, though I would be a moving target and I had no reason to believe she was a good shot. But if I did nothing, it was certain she'd shoot me. As many times as she needed to.

I looked over her shoulder, as though there was something out there, and said, "Oh my God."

She couldn't help herself; she looked over her shoulder. And as soon as she did, I rushed her. Bent over, my shoulder caught her in the gut. The gun went off, sending a wild shot into the air. My God it was loud. Something that surprises me every time. We both landed in the water which, thankfully, wasn't much colder than the air.

I tried standing up, but my feet were immediately pulled out from under me and I was underwater. As my arms were flapping around trying to pull me to the surface, a voice in my head said, 'Float.' I couldn't say why I knew that, I just did.

And since thrashing about didn't seem to be helping—and also hurt like hell—I let go, stopped moving, allowed myself to float. As my face broke the surface, I stretched my arms and legs out like a starfish. I was floating.

Not only was I floating, but I was also moving much more slowly than the current at the bottom. Stretching out my arms, I began pulling myself backward. I was doing a backstroke, and in only a minute or two I bumped into the dock. I grabbed onto it.

It was too tall for me to climb back onto it, so, holding tight, I put my feet onto the lake bottom and slowly made my way to shore. The rip current pulled at me the whole way, but I clung to the dock to make sure I didn't fall down and get pulled away again.

When I got to the stony beach, I looked out at the lake. I couldn't see Nancy Fisher anywhere. She wasn't flailing in the current, popping up and down, struggling not to drown. She was just gone.

It was time to call the sheriff—oh crap, I'd just been in the water, I was soaking wet, my phone—I reach for my pocket and it wasn't there. I patted myself down, but I didn't have it. Had it fallen out in the water? Or—wait, I remembered putting it down on the console in my car. And then I never picked it up. I ran—okay, walked relatively quickly out to the front of the house where my car was. Opening the door, I grabbed my phone and was about to dial 911 when it rang.

Edward.

"Hi, how are you?" I said when I clicked on. I might have sounded a little too cheerful. Near death experiences do that to me.

"I talked with Heartwell's. Dr. Blinski did put down bee sting on Ally's death certificate. I asked about a couple of other patients. He's been falsifying death certificates for quite a while."

"That makes sense. Um... I think I killed his nurse, Nancy Fisher."

"You think?"

"I knocked her into the water and I'm pretty sure she drowned."

"You murdered her? Is that what you're telling me?" I had the feeling this might be an even bigger problem in our relationship than my pill popping.

"She was holding a gun on me. She was going to kill me, so I knocked her into the water. Could you do me a favor? I've got to look for someone. Could you maybe call the sheriff for me? Send him to Nancy Fisher's?"

"Sure thing."

"Okay, talk to you later."

I popped my phone in my damp pocket and tried to wring out my shirt. Not very successful. I walked toward the house. I tried the front door. Not surprisingly, it was open. When would people up here learn? You should always lock your door, particularly if you're committing major felonies.

Walking through the living room, I was unable to stop myself from looking out at the lake. I half expected that Nancy would have popped up, that she hadn't just drowned, that she might be making her way out of the water. But, nope, she was dead. Definitely. Well, pretty sure.

In the empty kitchen, I looked around. Everything was very neat: dishes done, counters wiped, food put away. I heard Elbert call out, "Aunt Nancy?"

He'd heard me come in the front door. I walked around a corner and there was a door to the basement. I started down the steps. The basement was unfinished. As I walked down the steps, I could see a washer and dryer, a dusty exercise bike, a bench with tools. When I reached the bottom step, there was Ham tied to a chair. He was conscious, but there was a trail of blood across his forehead. He'd been walloped on the head.

Standing next to him—Elbert.

"Where's my aunt?"

"In Lake Michigan."

"Where's the gun?"

"Seriously? You're not going to ask if she's alive or dead, you're only worried about—oh, crap." Then I remembered she was wearing latex gloves. Someone else's fingerprints were on that gun. "That's Ronnie Sheck's gun, isn't it? You want to blame this whole thing on him, don't you? It's in Lake Michigan with your aunt."

"Fuck," he said. And then kept repeating the word.

Their plan became clear to me. They'd planned to shoot me and Hamlet with Ronnie Scheck's gun and then claim the reason he'd done it in Nancy's backyard was to try and blame her. Not a great plan but knowing the sheriff he'd have lapped it up.

I realized Elbert was frantically scanning the room. His eyes landed on the workbench. We both dove for it. He grabbed a hammer. I picked up a screwdriver. Not to put too fine a point on it, but I was probably screwed. A hammer seemed a lot more deadly. Plus, his arms were longer than mine. He took an immediate swing at me. I jumped back, then lunged forward with the screwdriver; missing him. He kept moving forward. Swinging. I kept jumping back, then lunging. This was not working out for me.

How long would it take the sheriff to get here? Hopefully, Edward told them I'd killed Nancy Fisher. That would make the sheriff really excited about getting here. On the other hand, I might be dead in the next sixty seconds.

I'd been backed into a wall. Which I didn't realize until I banged into something. I glanced back and saw it was a metal snow shovel hanging from a nail. I looked back at Elbert; the hammer was coming at me. I squatted quickly and he knocked the shovel off the wall. I dropped the screwdriver and grabbed the shovel instead, swinging it at him. It was flimsy so he just got bonked, but he did drop the hammer. Quickly, I kicked it away. Then bonked him again. And again. Bonk. Bonk. Bonk. Until we could hear the sirens.

"That's the sheriff. Are you going to behave or do I have to keep hitting you?"

Frankly, I was getting tired.

Elbert flipped over and crabbed away from me. He was on the other side of the basement when he began to cry.

"He killed Ally. I had to kill him. Had to."

He was sobbing; making sounds that I couldn't figure out. He was a messy crier. A lot of disgusting, saliva and dripping snot.

So gross.

CHAPTER TWENTY-TWO

My mother named my baby sister Emerald. Don't ask me why. I don't get the *Em* thing she and my grandmother have going on: Emma, Emily and now Emerald. And I don't understand why, since they're doing that, my name isn't Emmett. Or Emilio. Or Em...ward. Seriously, these people.

And the baby is fine. Perfectly healthy. Ten pounds, six ounces. My mother hadn't had any of the tests necessary for a woman of her age, no prenatal care (though at one point she mentioned taking vitamins 'for a while'), no ultrasounds, no monitoring, no exams... only she could ignore masses of helpful, information and medical advice, and still have a completely healthy child.

After she had Emerald, we had about twenty-four hours that were straight out of a happy, happy TV movie. Everything was all smiles and sunshine, and no one seemed to remember that we had serious, messy, awful dysfunctions.

I sat in my mother's hospital room, the baby at her breast, my nana sitting next to me. Three and a half generations in one room. And I told them the whole story of how I'd confronted Nancy and kind of killed her in self-defense. And then, how I'd saved Ham, Hamlet... honestly, it was more fun to say I'd saved Hamlet. No one in the play could say that.

I also told them how the sheriff spent about forty minutes screaming at me that he was going to put me in prison for killing poor Nancy until Detective Lehmann took him aside and reminded him of what self-defense was. Grumpily, the sheriff left me alone.

"Nana, when I was in the water. I had this idea that I should float. That I'd be safe if I stayed up at the surface. I don't know why I'd know something like that?"

"Don't you? That's your grandfather. The summer you were here, when you were twelve or thirteen, he took you out swimming several times. He would have told you how to deal with the rip currents."

"So, granddad saved me."

"Excuse me, I think I deserve some credit," my mother said. "I'm the one who sent you here that summer."

It was on the tip of my tongue to say, 'Dumped,' which was really more accurate and not something she should get credit for. But we were still in our happy, happy TV movie moment, so I didn't.

"Mother, could you remember to get formula."

"You're not going to breastfeed? Isn't that supposed to be better?" Yes, I spent far too much time reading articles on my Yahoo! homepage that had nothing to do with my life.

"Oh, doctors," she said. "You had formula. You survived."

I really didn't understand why she didn't understand that the bar for raising children should be a tad higher than mere survival.

When I'd had as much as I could take, I excused myself and wandered around the hospital until I found Ham, still in the ER. He was alone, dressed, and sitting on the edge of an exam table. When he saw me, he said, "They're letting me out soon."

"How's your head?"

"It feels like the morning after nine scotches and two packs of cigarettes."

I hadn't done exactly that, but I had done similar things, so I said, "Ouch."

"Thank you for saving me."

"You're welcome. Random question: Why do you think they didn't just shoot you? Why were you still alive?"

"They weren't sure you'd come. They figured they might need me to get you there."

"That didn't work out to well."

"It did for me. Say, are you really going back to Los Angeles?" he asked.

"Totally. As soon as I can."

"That's a shame."

"Have you looked around? I don't exactly fit in here."

"Well, yeah, but... It's been hard being up here for two weeks. I have clients in Grand Rapids screaming their heads off. I could really use someone in the area."

"You mean me? I'm not a private investigator. I don't have a license."

"You don't need a license. You can work for me. As an investigator. If you put in enough hours and take a test, you can get a license. If that's important to you."

It wasn't. Exactly. And I wouldn't be here long enough—

"That's really flattering. I appreciate the offer. But I'm not going to be here."

"Got it."

"I guess Helena wants some of her money back."

"Helena only paid for the first week. Your grandmother paid for the second week. She wanted me to keep an eye on you."

Wow. I was instantly furious. Not that Nana Cole thought I needed looking after, I probably did, but Ham charged twenty-five hundred dollars a week. Eventually, she'd try to make me pay her back.

"Is something wrong?" Ham asked.

"Nothing's wrong. And it's all wrong."

"Ah, yeah. Life."

THE NEXT AFTERNOON, I went to see Detective Lehmann. At his request. He brought me into their interview room and closed the door. He didn't beat around the bush.

"Elbert Robins says he didn't stab you. But he's confessed to everything else, so I kind of believe him."

Okay, that was not good. That left one strong possibility—

"Sue Langtree," he said.

"What about her?"

"She stabbed you."

"Really?"

Honestly, it wasn't a surprise. I was pretty sure she regretted confessing to me that she'd killed Reverend Hessel.

"Are you just guessing?"

"I met with Donny Hyslip. Made him an offer. If he confessed to raping Bekah Springer I wouldn't prosecute him for murder. He was smart about it and confessed."

"Okay."

"So you see, there's no reason to protect Sue Langtree."

And there wasn't.

"Have you been able to connect her to the shirt you found at Donny Hyslip's?"

"It's vintage, right?"

"Yeah. It belonged to Sue's husband. She's got a bunch. She wears them when she gardens. You should look at her photo albums. She might have a photo of her husband wearing the shirt."

"Good point. Thank you."

"And the paperweight. She collects them. The one that was used to kill Reverend Hessel, she gave to him. She took it home at first. It was in her living room until she planted it on Donny Hyslip. I saw it there."

"And you'll testify to that?"

"I don't know if I'll be around."

"You don't know if you'll be alive or in Masons Bay?"

"Masons Bay. Come on, give me a break."

"It would be good if you'd testify."

"You want to fly me from L.A., I'll think about it."

"We might be able to do without you for Sue, but we'll definitely need you for the Ruperts."

The Ruperts being my distant cousins who'd murdered Sammy Hart and tried to kill me. Twice.

"Didn't they confess?"

"Recanted."

"What do they say happened?"

"You attacked them."

"Seriously? In my own backyard?"

"We're going to need you to testify."

"When is the trial?"

"January, February. Maybe longer. And then there's Elbert Robins. He hasn't taken a deal yet."

This wasn't particularly fair. I was the victim, after all. This should really be a whole lot easier.

"How are you feeling?" Detective Lehmann asked.

I was not feeling well. The Vicodin my grandmother had been giving me had run out. So now, in addition to pain, I was beginning to feel nauseated and chilled, and I had a bad headache coming on. I needed to stop at the pharmacy and get my prescription for Ativan filled.

But what I really wanted to do was drive out to Ronnie Sheck's and pick up some Oxy. I'd keep titrating down, I promised myself, but I wasn't ready to just stop. Too much had happened. Too much was going to happen. I needed someone in my corner. Oxycontin was always in my corner.

The irony of sitting in the sheriff's office deciding that I was definitely going to leave and make a drug deal was not lost on me. But that's what life is, a series of zigs and zags that never exactly fit together.

"I asked how you're feeling," Detective Lehmann said.

"Oh, right. I'm okay. Considering."

"Do you have health insurance?"

"Do I look like I have health insurance?"

"No. You don't. Look, the state has a victim's fund. You might qualify for some money. Plus, they might have some ideas about how you can negotiate with the hospital."

"Okay. Thanks."

Neither of us said anything for a minute, then I said, "I need to go."

Score some drugs. And that's what I did.

CHAPTER TWENTY-THREE

When I got home, it was almost time for Nana Cole and me to go to the hospital and pick up my mother and baby sister. I'd taken half a ten. Still titrating. Not enough to be impaired, just enough to not go into withdrawal. Everything was going to be fine.

But when I got home, the Escalade was gone. That didn't make sense. My grandmother couldn't drive at the moment. Maybe she had Bev take her to the hospital to get my mother, but, if so... where was Bev's Jeep? The whole thing was weird.

I got out of my car. My lovely car that was going to drive me, slowly, out to California. After giving the cloth roof a pat, I walked to the back of the house and went in through the back door. Nana Cole was standing next to the stove holding a pink bundle, Emerald, in one hand, while gripping her cane in the other. A bottle was warming in a pan.

"Where's your car?" I asked.

"I gave it to your mother."

"Gave—how did she get home from the hospital? I thought we were going to get her?"

"She took a cab. We have them, you know."

"And then you gave her the car to—what? Go to Benson's? Should she be doing that? She just had a baby?"

"She's not at Benson's."

"Where is she?"

"Not sure. She thought it was better if we don't know."

"Excuse me? She's gone? Like, *gone* gone? Like not coming back gone? And you let her steal your car?"

"I gave her my car."

There was so much wrong with this conversation. First, my mother was gone—and my baby sister was not. Also, Nana Cole gave her a very expensive SUV; all she'd ever given me was a bill.

About then, I'd had enough of my grandmother hovering my infant sister over the stove.

"Give her to me," I said, holding out my arms.

"Be careful of her head," she said.

"Seriously? I know. They say that in every TV show ever. It's the one thing I actually know about babies."

When I had Emerald nestled in my arms, I said to Nana Cole, "Sit down."

I must have said that very sternly, because she did what I said without any complaint.

"These are the rules. Number one: You do not try to walk and carry a baby at the same time. Not while you're using a cane. Number two: You're going to call the physical therapist and have her come help you until *she* says you can walk and carry a baby at the same time."

"But—"

"No buts. If you drop this baby, I will wring your neck!"

Okay that was weird. I'll admit, it wasn't the first time I'd threatened my grandmother with violence; it was, however, the first time I'd done it for someone else. I put Emerald back in her arms. She fussed a bit, but she didn't cry.

"How do I know when the formula is ready?"

"It needs to be warm but not hot."

I took the bottle out of the water and nearly burned my fingers off. "Okay, I think this is too hot." I walked over to the sink and ran the cold water. I dipped the bottle under a few times. Then I squirted about a teaspoon onto my wrist and didn't get third degree burns so it was probably okay. I handed the bottle to my grandmother. She popped it into the baby's mouth.

"She's so tiny," I couldn't help saying.

"Henry, she's enormous. It can take some babies three months to weigh ten pounds."

That didn't mean she wasn't tiny. I mean, seriously, ten pounds?

"Where did she go?" I asked.

"I told you; I don't know."

"You didn't ask?"

"Of course, I didn't ask. She'd have just lied. I don't need to be lied to. She's done enough of that already."

"I can't believe you're this calm."

"It's not like she hasn't done this before. Who do you think took care of you for the first year of your life?"

"My mother?"

"No. Me." She was looking down at Emerald when she said, "She looks like she's going to be a good eater. That's always a good thing. You were fussy and difficult."

Don't say it. I still am. I know.

"You have no idea when she'll come back?" I asked.

"None whatsoever. I know she will though. She came back for you. I almost didn't give you back. But she needed you."

There was something disturbing about that, which I didn't want to think about. "I'm going to go to the bathroom," I said. "Don't move until I get back, all right?"

"I'm fine."

I walked down to the bathroom. Closing the door behind me, I was trying to decide. Should I take a half 10? Or should I just take a whole 10? I really needed a whole 10. Wanted it bad.

How could my mother do something like this? Leaving a two-day-old infant with an invalid and an addict. Oh crap. I was the addict she shouldn't have left a baby with. I had to... that had to change. Shit. Fuck. God damn it. I dumped the Oxy I'd just bought an hour before into the toilet. Then flushed.

I called Bev and Barbara to come over and help my mother with Emerald while I ran a couple of errands. While I waited for them to get there, I asked Nana Cole, "Do you need anything else for the baby?"

"I don't think so. Most of what we need is boxed up on the porch."

"My baby things," I guessed. Not my mother's like I'd assumed.

"Yes."

I looked over my grandmother's shoulder at Emerald. She was ten and a half pounds of lumpy pink flesh. Seriously, she didn't amount to much when it came down to it. But I'd just thrown away fifteen Oxys for her. And I knew that I wouldn't let anything happen to her. That I didn't want her to grow up the way I had, bounced around, parked here and there. Ignored one minute, gushed over the next. I knew that in order to protect her, I couldn't take drugs. Like, at all.

Bev and Barbara got there pretty quickly and started cooing over Emerald. They barely asked where my mother was. They'd known my grandmother for a long time. I guess there wasn't much about this situation that was a surprise to anyone except me.

I drove to the pharmacy next to Benson's and had my prescription for Ativan filled. I took one in the car. I looked at my flip phone; four-fifty. I was going to be late.

Behind Cheswick Community Church there is a large pole barn that's partly finished inside. I'd been there once for a pancake breakfast. There was a circle of folding chairs in the center of the large room. Most of the chairs were full. I took one of the two empty ones. I tried not to look at anyone.

The meeting had already started, probably a while before. It had taken me longer to get out of the car than it had to drive there from Masons Bay. But I had gotten out and went inside.

This older guy, who I thought might have been one of the cashiers at Bensons, was talking about how he used to steal from everyone, including the store where he worked. When he was done everyone applauded. I didn't quite get it. All he'd done was admit he was a thief. Something that was probably not a good idea at all.

"Thank you for sharing, Raymond," a woman in her mid-fifties said. She wore a big, sloppy blouse and black tights. "We have a newcomer. Thank you for joining us. I'm Tammy and I'm an addict. Would you like to tell us your name?"

"Mooch."

There was an awkward pause while everyone waited. I knew I was supposed to say I was an addict, but I could barely admit it to myself. I didn't want to say something like that to entire room full of people. Finally, they said, "Hello, Mooch."

Then the meeting continued. They 'shared' that they'd done terrible things to get drugs; had sex with people they didn't like, stolen from people they did like, broken laws—beyond just drug laws, manipulated family members into giving them 'loans' they never paid back... the whole thing was interminable. And I had no clue why this was supposed to be helping me.

Finally, they ran out of woes to complain about. Then, shockingly, Tammy looked at me, and said, "Mooch, in case you didn't pick up on it, we're talking about the worst things drugs ever made us do. I know you're new, and maybe you're just visiting, but would you like to share the worst thing drugs ever made you do?"

I looked around the room, their expressions were expectant, hopeful. They couldn't wait to hear what I had to say. I took a deep breath. I had to tell the truth; even though it was my first visit I knew this process didn't tolerate anything else. So, truthfully, the worst thing I'd ever done because of drugs was...

"This."

ABOUT THE AUTHOR

Marshall Thornton writes several popular mystery series, most notably the *Boystown Mysteries* and the *Pinx Video Mysteries*. He has won the Lambda Award for Gay Mystery three times. His books *Femme* and *Code Name Liberty* were Lambda finalists for Best Gay Romance. Other books include *My Favorite Uncle*, *The Ghost Slept Over* and *Fathers of the Bride*. He holds an MFA in Screenwriting from UCLA.

ALSO BY MARSHALL THORNTON

IN THE BOYSTOWN MYSTERIES SERIES

The Boystown Prequels
(Little Boy Dead & Little Boy Afraid)
Boystown: Three Nick Nowak Mysteries
Boystown 2: Three More Nick Nowak Mysteries
Boystown 3: Two Nick Nowak Novellas
Boystown 4: A Time for Secrets
Boystown 5: Murder Book
Boystown 6: From the Ashes
Boystown 7: Bloodlines
Boystown 8: The Lies That Bind
Boystown 9: Lucky Days
Boystown 10: Gifts Given
Boystown 11: Heart's Desire
Boystown 12: Broken Cord
Boystown 13: Fade Out

IN THE PINX VIDEO MYSTERIES SERIES

Night Drop
Hidden Treasures
Late Fees
Rewind
Cash Out
Help Wanted

OTHER BOOKS

The Perils of Praline

Desert Run

Full Release

The Ghost Slept Over

My Favorite Uncle

Femme

Praline Goes to Washington

Aunt Belle's Time Travel & Collectibles

Masc

Never Rest

Year of the Rat

Fathers of the Bride

A Mean Season

Sentenced to Christmas

www.ingramcontent.com/pod-product-compliance
Lightning Source LLC
Chambersburg PA
CBHW021154310726
48971CB00002B/623